WAGER

❧BOOK 7❧

BLENDED

WAGER

Copyright ©2018 Erica Chilson

Wicked Reads
PO Box 29
Nelson, PA 16940

www.ericachilson.com/wicked-reads

Printed in the United States of America

First Printing, 2018

ISBN-13: **978-0-9979899-9-1**
ISBN-10: **0-9979899-9-8**

Titles by Erica Chilson

Mistress and Master of Restraint

Restraint
Unleashed
Dexter
Dalton
Queen Omnibus*
Jaded*
Queened*
Checkmate*
King
Faithless
The Hunter
Integrated

BLENDED

Good Girl
Wildly Wedded Wife
Widow
Wanton
Warped
Woven
Wager
Wicked

RUSTY KNOB

Rusty Knob
Tarnished
Stainless
Polished

The Kline family has taken over Fairport... Devon knows himself too well, how he'll be up in their business, taking on their problems, and no one can have that catastrophe happen.

Scheming, Devon manages to convince Rory and Beth to take another honeymoon to Las Vegas for the weekend, using it as an excuse for Essie and Devon to finally have a honeymoon of their own too– all smoke and mirrors to get the four of them out of Fairport during Auggie's intervention.

But Devon has met his match in the manipulating schemes department– since the playground, Bethany and Devon have always butted heads over who got to boss Essie around. Now that Rory has rejoined their group, Beth is determined to come to an agreement with Devon, one which will blow his mind.

Stuck on a six-hour flight, there is no escaping Beth for Devon. By the time the wheels touch down on the runway, Devon's views on life, love, and their futures have dramatically changed.

Are Devon, Beth, Rory, and Essie willing to wager a lifetime of contentment to chase the chance for an unexpectedly thrilling happily ever after?

WAGER

~BOOK 7~

BLENDED

CHAPTER ONE

Devon Mason

Watching our wives conspire, as they wind their way down the hallway toward the club proper, "Hmm... I feel abandoned for some reason," Rory mutters wryly, leaning against the wall next to me.

The man distracts me so much, I almost miss my dad sneaking past us, leaving the bathroom. I hate the defeated curl to Dad's shoulders and the way his head slopes forward on his neck. But Delaney made me promise to be selfish enough to only worry about how I'm feeling, or how I make others feel. In a few years, maybe I can graduate to being the helpful one, when I don't take on their pain as my own.

Rory is so in tune with my emotional climate, he senses what's riding beneath the surface without me having to utter a single word. Just as Essie and I have similarities and major differences in our personalities, Rory and Bethany do too. Their only commonality is how accurately they can read people, especially me, added to their insane need to offer assistance.

Leaning into me, Rory's warmth chases some of the icy fear away. "I could probably bribe Jim at the speedway to let us race our cars after closing. You in?" With another nudge, he's grinning down at me.

Never one to be at the disadvantage in any given situation, I try not to show how Rory rocks my world. "My plan's more fun," I murmur slyly, lips curling into a knowing smirk.

Earlier this week, I overheard Dad on the phone with Patrick Kline, Auggie's dad, and my mind began spinning plots on how to get the hell out of Fairport for the weekend. Currently, Auggie's at the bar, surrounded by meddling family– *don't I know it!* The whole Kline family is in attendance, from the pastor grandfather, right down to the youngest Kline– Auggie's uncle, Toby.

There are parts of me that can never be silenced by a mood stabilizer cocktail, no matter how consummate of an actor I may be. Auggie is my uncle, twice over, by being my dad's pseudo-stepbrother and my aunt's boyfriend. I've been around the entire Kline family my whole life, so much so, I feel as if I'm a part of the family. Being left out has me hankering to help, to an unhealthy degree. My sanity has me running to the nearest airport.

I hurt for Auggie, even if most days I want to smash his face in, and I worry no differently than the rest of them. Auggie needs a wakeup call, because he's driving us all nuts. I can sympathize, because I've been there– torturing your loved ones but being unable to stop yourself, mixed with the suffocating panic of an intervention.

Half of you feels you deserve having your ass handed to you by your nearest and dearest, but the other half believes you don't deserve help either.

Rory and Beth's reception is the meeting place for the intervention, but it will be moving to the Spook House shortly, which is why Dad looks so defeated. He'll be joining them– just Dad.

There's a bunch of secrets that are killing Auggie, and if anyone understands how toxic that can be, it's me. Lisa, Auggie's mom, she organized this entire clusterfuck, even bringing in some bigshot IRS agent from New York– some guy who's bossing Toby around these days –to mediate the intervention. No doubt Dexter Hayes will get the job done, because the little dude even terrifies me, and that's saying something.

I've got to get out of here before I end up at the bar, sticking my nose where I think it belongs, taking on other people's problems I can't solve, when I've got my own shit to figure out. I need to be distracted in a big motherfucking way.

Jarring me out of my toxic thoughts, "Enlighten me," Rory challenges, bumping me with his elbow.

I feel it happening, just as I do every time, but there's nothing that can stop my eyes from doing that fluttery dumbshit look I'm always giving the guy. Rory makes my brain short-circuit and my skin quiver with the need to be touched, but there's a forbidden edge to it Essie can't give me.

This thing between Rory and me, it feels so naughty, so right yet wrong by society's standards– it chases the shadows away and lights up my veins better than my favorite intravenous drugs.

I need to get the hell out of Fairport, but I'm not going anywhere without my drug of choice. Deciding this is the best segue, "I didn't have a honeymoon–"

"You didn't want one, if memory serves right." No judgement or condemnation, Rory just understands why I couldn't do a shit-show of a wedding.

I didn't want a huge wedding, like we're innocent virgins with a squeaky-clean past. I may be cynical, but I prefer realistic. They would've shown up to gossip. The drug addict lunatic, the pregnant town whore, getting married with their victims surrounding them, with the girl they both scorned standing up as one of their witnesses.

If only they knew how Rory and I were messing around, that would just add fuel to the townsfolk's torches.

Call me paranoid, if you want, but I'm a realist. I'm not narcissistic enough to think people actually give a fuck. People don't want to waste their fucking time, money, and energy to attend a wedding– they just don't. Unless they're immediate family, or the best of friends, it's an obligation they wish they could get out of. Everything out of their mouths are lies, as they compare and judge everything at the wedding. While everyone else is wondering what the score is on the game, sneaking looks at their cellphones.

All a huge wedding does is feed egos, empty bank accounts, and make people feel like shit because their grandiose gesture wasn't as big as the next person's over-the-top bullshit. It gets the women fighting, because their friend or relative is loved more because they spent more on an event that lasts a few hours in a lifetime. Then the men feel like shit because they didn't waste money on empty bullshit gestures.

Romance is fake.

Real love makes you want to motherfucking puke your guts out in terror, but it makes you feel alive unlike nothing else on the planet.

Instead of putting on a show for the town gossips, Essie and I are putting our time, money, and effort into making our marriage work and paying our bills, so we can have a better life.

What about the wedding gifts?

Realist.

The anti-attention-whore.

The cost far outweighs the gifts we didn't need. We didn't need five hand-mixers, or fine china, or monogrammed towel sets, or a dozen punch bowls. We live in a house dubbed the Shithole– let's face it, we don't entertain, and we ought to be fixing said shithole instead of wasting money to fill the fondue pots we'll never use.

When you average out the price per plate for a catered reception, we shouldn't tax our families to help pay for a wedding, while begging our friends and family to give us gifts they can't afford.

Everyone loses, except for the wedding and reception venue, the caterer, and the slew of services we'd have to hire, while fueling the town gossip.

Essie understood how five minutes after the wedding no one would care whether we spent a grand or a hundred grand, but our baby needs a college fund, we needed vehicles, we need a new roof, and we both need some breathing room in our bank accounts.

As for a honeymoon, I did want that, wanted to experience it with Essie and our best friends, and have the pictures to go with the memories. We've been busy... I've made time.

Right now.

"You went to Vegas for yours, but it couldn't have been any fun." Even though I was locked in a mental health facility at the time, I'm still jealous I wasn't around to experience this with Beth and Rory. Then the guilt hits– Essie was left all alone because Beth and I were selfish assholes. "I mean, Beth had no one to shop with, and you had no one to gamble with. I'm sure the sex was fantastic, but you needed more fun than that."

"Oh, yeah?" Rory biting his bottom lip draws my gaze, eyes lasering on the way his crooked front tooth leaves an indent. He's trying to stifle the laughter threatening to erupt, but it's a sexual sight for me. Skin boiling, I quickly look away, imagining those same teeth leaving indents in every inch of my flesh… in Beth's– in Essie's.

Turning sheepish, fearing Rory won't bend to my will as usual, "So I bought you a gift–"

"Like my pants?" Rory banters with me, smile evident in his voice.

"Exactly like the pants," I volley back, smirking smugly. Rory has no idea how the soft cotton forms around his junk as he walks– I could tell he was free-balling it. Everyone inside Rush has been staring, coveting the flesh that's mine.

My possessive streak erupting is another reason I've got to get the hell out of Rush. I'm having a hard time hiding my reactions, and I refuse to share with anyone but the girls.

I'm a great actor, but every time someone looks at Rory's swinging junk, I get an inch closer to reaching out and swatting their faces. I keep telling everyone I'm still me, and I am, medicated and enlightened or not.

Murmuring sheepishly to hide my possessive thoughts, "The gift was to you, but more for me."

"So what gift did you get yourself this time?" Expression bright and open, Rory takes my breath away.

I've been struggling to admit what's been going on inside my head, even with my therapists. My child-self fell in love with Essie, and it's a bond that will never break– a similar one forged between Rory and Beth way back then too. I can't imagine a life without Essie in it, without waking up in the middle of the night with her back pressed against my chest and the soothing sound of her soft snores. I recognize the same intimacy when Rory looks at Beth, the way his voice subtly changes, and the way Beth looks back at Rory.

I still lie. All the time. But never to myself anymore.

I barely stop myself from harming Beth sometimes in a jealous fit of rage, and she can read it too. Beth and I are too similar, because I know she's thought the same thoughts, but we both want Rory to be happy more than we want to tear each other to bits.

On the playground, we used to fight over who got to boss Essie around. Beth will lie, but she was relieved when I walked away during our teenage years. Our fight at the playground, the night Beth told me Essie was pregnant, was yet another power struggle over who loved Essie best. We've come to an agreement on Essie... we're going to have to have a talk about Rory.

This insanity I feel can't be altered by meds– the way I want to puke yet laugh...

I'm falling in love as an adult, and it's utterly terrifying– the most thrilling thing I've ever encountered.

"Four tickets to Vegas," I ramble off quickly, emotions warring between worrying I'll be rejected and fearing Rory can read how much I need him. "Leaving tonight."

"Holy shit!" Gasping in wonder, Rory stares at me like I'm too good to be true, which is how I feel every time I look at him. "For real?"

"Vegas is filled with stimulation that requires no stimulants." Holding my eyes wide, I try to stop my dumbass eyelashes from fluttering again, but it happens anyway. "I want to have fun. Live."

Quivering in a mix of nervousness and that punch to the guts love-sickness sensation, Rory recognizes I'm on the cusp of a freak out. "Devon?"

"Yeah?" I whisper, trying to get my emotions under control, but failing miserably.

"You trust me, right?" Rory's tone is measured, even and low, a sound that instantly has the panic receding. Relaxing, I nod, unable to voice the chaotic stew of emotions I have for this man. "I vow that you will have something to look forward to– *every single day* –for the next seventy years."

Unrepentantly shameless, not even bothering to see if anyone is looking, I lean up to steal a quick kiss. Floating, while trying to keep my feet firmly on the ground, I can't wipe the grin of satisfaction off my face.

"And I promise to always keep you guessing, keep our life interesting." Still grinning, smug tone following behind me, I grab for Rory's arm, then pull him down the hallway toward the party in full-swing.

Part of me is testing Rory– always testing, testing everyone about everything. It's a major facet of my personality, not a factor in my mental illness. Everyone assumes my negative behaviors can be righted by meds, but not when it's the core of who I am.

I test, but I no longer issue tests where no one can win.

The test is to see if Rory will reject me by pulling away. Asshole that I am, I do this during his wedding reception to someone other than me. My hard-hitting tests always put people on the spot, wedge them into impossible situations.

Selfish dick that I am, I know Essie will follow my lead. It may be Beth I have to fear as an adversary, but it's Rory's emotions that terrify me the most.

The townsfolk got nothing on how terrifying it's been worrying about whether or not Rory could ever accept this new lifestyle... could ever love me back.

The most ironic song blasts from the strategically placed speakers around Rush. Blood in the Cut by K. Flay. The lyrics filter into my mind, specific parts punching me in the junk.

The boy I love's got another girl... guess I'm contagious– it'd be safer if you ran... take my arm, break it in half. Say something, do it soon... I need noise. I need the buzz of a sub. Need the crack of a whip. Need some blood in the cut... I need blood in the cut... I need blood in the cut... Met back up with the boy I love. Cried on the streets of San Francisco. I don't have an agenda. All I do is pretend to be okay, so my friends can't see my heart is in a blender.

Fingers clenching around Rory's forearm, I pull us into the thick of the action, bodies pressing from every side on the dance floor. The heat is oppressive, but it sends a chill down my spine. The deafening music has sweat beading along the nape of my neck. The crush of bodies has anxiety twitching my fingertips.

I know every person in this club, yet it's stifling, panic-inducing. But with Rory, I feel safe, and that's a feeling I can't get from my wife, when it's me who was born to protect her.

Being a strong alpha male doesn't mean we don't have insecurities and fears, that we don't panic, or that we know everything. I can protect myself and my wife, until I can't– there are dark nightmares that I cannot escape. Nightmares Beth can walk me through. Nightmares Rory can protect and comfort me from. Taking care of Essie returns the masculinity the nightmares took away from me in the first place.

I need them.

I'm broken in a way that conventional society will call me a freak, when I voice what I need to survive. I'm not normal, and I'm good with that, because the only thing I want to do is live, no matter the cost to my reputation.

"Congratulations, Rory!" Nina pats Rory's broad chest, small hand resting on his shirt, and I swallow down the need to mark my territory.

I enjoy misunderstood Nina, but love is turning me into an irrational shit. Everyone will think my meds are off balance as I plateau into a manic phase, when it's my very real emotions ruling me.

There's a need to run– not away but toward –where Beth and Essie are chatting animatedly to Willow and Ren, while tugging Rory forcefully behind me.

As irrational as it may seem, the four of us need to be together, the drive suffocating me.

Impatient, I grip Rory's arm tighter, knowing no one notices how we're touching. When what I truly want to do is to lace our fingers together, raise our clasped hands over my head, then shout above the pounding music how Rory is mine, during a party celebrating Rory's union with Beth.

I've had half a dozen mental double-takes since I stepped foot into Rush tonight, but I'm just going to roll with it. It's love, not insanity, even if love makes me feel insane.

"It's nice to see you," I mumble quickly to Nina, not touching her for two reasons. One, I'm not big on the touchy feely with randoms. Two, Nina and my father are oil and water, no matter how cordial Dad is to her. I'm a shrunken version of Dad, even if we act nothing alike, so I skeeve out poor Nina.

"Have a good night, Nina," I say in parting, cutting Rory off before he starts his chatter.

Rory's a social butterfly, but we don't have time for that right now. I may not be able to hear Rory's laughter, but I can feel it vibrating down my arm, and I can see it lighting his face in the darkened club as the strobe flickers across his satisfied grin.

Proving he's stronger than I am, Rory yanks me to a stop, somehow managing to control my feet. "So impatient," Rory whispers in my ear, lips fluttering against my flesh, breath scorching.

Cock hardening, my eyelashes flutter. Anyone looking could never mistake the expression on my face for anything other than longing hunger.

"Let's kidnap our girls," Rory says at an audible level, mouth no longer touching me. Taking advantage of my stunned silence, he slides by me, body rubbing against mine, two layers of soft cotton the only barrier against our stiffness caressing each other.

Taking charge, Rory pulls me through Rush by his grip on my wrist. Expression open, friendly and welcome, as he nods and smiles at everyone we pass, but his swift stride speaks a story of impatience and need.

Anxiety mixing with arousal, the press of bodies heightens the sensory overload. The instant we get within arm's reach of the girls, my mouth is fused to Essie's. Breathless, passionate, I flood my wife with all the emotions inundating me, allowing her to siphon it off.

Uncomfortable laughter spills into my mouth, Essie's confused as I suck her down into me, with a crowded club of our friends and family watching on.

The kiss is meant for Essie, but it's also for Rory. It's socially acceptable to kiss your own wife, even if it's a kiss best reserved for the marital bed, versus devouring the groom's tongue during his reception to a bride, who most certainly isn't me.

Nerves on edge, I pull away, shaking slightly, satisfied by how Essie's pupils are blown. My wife craves being wanted, and I want her and want everyone else to recognize it. Even as another man holds onto my wrist... even as I still hunger to kiss him with the same intensity, still want everyone to recognize he's mine too.

Eyes reaching out, I connect with Beth's calm yet assertive gaze, begging her to help me– anchor me before I lose myself.

Smiling as if nothing is going on between us, Beth reaches out to tug me closer, not looking odd since we're in a packed, loud club, and it's usual for a friend to whisper in another's ear to be heard above the pounding beat.

"We need to talk," Beth's words belie the reassuring expression on her face. "I hear we have a long flight– one where you can't escape me."

CHAPTER TWO

Life is thrilling when you're surrounded by people who make it worth living. The tedious tasks are suddenly fun, like sitting around an airport, when every other time you'd rather put a bullet through your skull than wait.

With Essie, Rory, and Beth at my side, standing in line for a green tea for me, two sugary Frappuccinos for the girls, and a black coffee for Rory was more than tolerable, more like fun as we chatted in excitement. Picking out t-shirts with **Massachusetts** embossed across the front, while snapping ridiculous selfies, were memories in the making, instead of the boredom I felt when my brothers made me suffer through the same a few years back.

Phone in my pocket, sitting in a dank seat where many asses have sat before, I'm perfectly content– happy even. Watching Rory and Essie talking nonstop, barely letting the other finish before they're replying, is one of the most entertaining experiences of my life. Beth is equally quiet, soaking in their conversation rather than engaging in it.

Even a root canal would be amazing as long as my best friends were with me, and this is coming from someone who always sees the negative side of things, a person who stresses the pain instead of the life lesson.

Beth and I have always had that silent conversation thing down pat, even when we were feeling bitter and jealous of the other. The dread of the not-so silent conversation to come doesn't even dampen the excitement of it all.

The major drawback to there being four of us is how there aren't four side-by-side seats on the plane. I'd stressed for a few hours when I booked the flight, not sure who to place next to whom. I settled with seating us with our respective partners, even if I longed to sit with Rory too.

Beth warned we'd be talking on the flight, and I'd felt a thrill of satisfaction of thwarting her plan due to our seating arrangement. Essie and I were seated together, with Essie at the window, and across the aisle from me was Rory, then Beth.

All those years in school have paid off for Beth, because she had our tickets switched, to where I'm stuck in the window seat with Beth blocking my exit to the aisle, with Essie and Rory sitting together in the aisle section.

Beth's smiling serenely as she gazes at Rory and Essie animatedly chattering about the success of the party they planned, but she's also watching me in her periphery. The gleam in Beth's eye is anticipatory.

The trepidation can't overpower the excitement I'm feeling, even with Beth challenging me with her stare.

Our rows are called, and the four of us get up, giddily chattering and sharing connecting touches, embarking on another journey of our shared honeymoon.

My mind roils as we stow our carry-ons and find our seats, thinking over how I don't see this as Essie's and my honeymoon, or a second honeymoon for Rory and Beth. A euphoric part of me feels as if this is *our* honeymoon. The four of us. Together. No matter how irrational that sounds, even inside my own head.

Several people brush up against my back on their way down the aisle, causing every muscle to lock in my body. Frozen still, my arms are raised to push Essie's carry-on into the upper cabinet. Person after person jostles me as they move down the aisle like cattle– their scents, their sounds, the way they move their bodies, all of it turning my stomach.

No doubt sensing my imminent freak-out, Rory reaches up to stow the bag, his bag going in after it. Hand lowering, he rubs the small of my back, large fingers splaying along my hip. "Good luck," Rory breathes into my ear, then sinks into his seat, laughter not fading as my wife sits next to him.

Essie grins up at me, flashing the cat that ate the canary smile I generally wear, which means she's been plotting with her BFF again– hell, I get the feeling Rory's been plotting with them both too.

Three-against-one, not fair odds, that.

"You'll pay for this," I warn the pair of sneaky snakes, eyes connecting with both of theirs in turn. Their laughter fills my ears as I shuffle to sit in the window seat. Then Beth's there, her womanly body offering me no room for escape.

Beth makes me wait, all calm and sure, as the flight attendants do their usual bullshit before takeoff. In a panic, not a single one of us is going to remember the spiel. A cosmic joke– our seats as floatation devices –when we're flying over the bulk of the continental US, with its mountains, plains, and heat-baked deserts… with no deep bodies of water in sight.

The seat is already killing my back and ass, no way in hell is it going to cushion my landing, most likely somewhere over the Midwest.

Fingertips gripping my thighs, no doubt leaving bruises behind, the freak-out is no longer imminent. The sweats. The fingertip twitches. The laundry list of nervous system and mental tics.

Sounds rush in, mixing until I cannot single out one from the mass of others– men and women speaking too loudly, causing others to talk even louder, until they're in a competition to see who can get the most attention by being heard by those who don't give two shits about Timmy's missing sippy cup. For once, the older the person, the ruder they become, with sullen teenagers ignoring us all.

Scents sting my nostrils– the smell of unwashed bodies, dirty diapers and spit-up, too many perfumes fighting colognes, all covering natural stench. Ass and piss and disgusting foods, all fusing together into an overpowering mix, thanks to the stale, moldy air being circulated in the aircraft.

Pressure. Increasing pressure, until my ears threaten to burst. Swallowing. Swallowing. Swallowing. Just as we reach altitude, my ears finally pop, offering a bit of relief, if you can call being able to hear several screaming babies relief.

Closing my eyes, I'm thankful nothing is touching me as my other senses are assaulted. The last flight I took was pure torture. My skin becomes more sensitive as my mind tries to balance out all my senses. The soft cotton on my back and ass are a comfort, but the back-killing seat and the gut-pinching belt are where I place my focus.

Another cry joins the fray, this time from a toddler directly behind me, sitting on its mother's lap. A tiny hand pummels the back of my head, fingertip snagging my hair to tear out several strands.

Skin crawling off my muscles, I suck in a deep breath, trying to control my emotions, because the fight-or-flight reflex is a hairsbreadth from erupting.

Since I'm stuck on a flight, a bazillion feet from solid ground, and the seat belt sign is still on, escaping to the nearest, dinky bathroom is out of the question... that leaves fight as my only option, but it's a toddler assaulting me.

I love kids of all ages– I understand them more than I understand adults. It's the mother who is shouting at her child, ten decibels louder than the toddler's cries, that will be the target of my self-defense.

Don't adults remember what it was like to be children? That toddler is scared, its ears are hurting, and its mother is shouting at it as if it's doing something wrong, when all it's trying to do is communicate in the only way it knows how. The toddler is feeding off its mother's panic, when it needs to be soothed and reassured.

"Here." Beth pries my fingertips off my thigh, and I'm thankful I changed into a pair of pants for the flight, or else I would have bloodied my bare skin. "Focus on this."

A squishy ball is pressed into my palm, fingers instantly sinking deep into the foam. With my eyes still shut, I know exactly which toy this is, by touch alone. A slight smile curls my lips, a chuckle of relief threatening to escape my mouth, even as the mother's voice behind me pitches higher in frustration.

Rory may be across the aisle, with Essie and Beth between us, but he's still with me. This ball is his– a cheesy pink heart, of all things. A private joke Rory played on me, carrying a pocketful of balls to match my moods.

A cartoonish, grublike dick, for when I'm being a dick.

A pair of squishy boobs, for when I'm acting like a child, crying out for its mother's milk.

A keychain shaped like a Fleshlight, for when I'm clingy, handsy, or irritably horny.

A small Grumpy Cat stuffed keychain– that's self-explanatory.

An angry poop foam stress ball– also self-explanatory.

A squishy heart for when Rory wants to comfort me with his representation of a hug.

"Better?" Beth breathes into my ear, hand rubbing the back of my neck. My seat lurches forward as the toddler freaks out worse, its mother's voice going hoarse from shouting. A flight attendant is smiling falsely, palm landing lightly on seatbacks as she answers questions while walking down the aisle toward us, with the commotion as her destination.

A fight with my seatbelt ensues, and I can tell Beth is terrified as to why I'm struggling to get free, by the way her breath hitches slightly. Takes a lot to get the girl to freak out on me and yell, but I'm the only one who ever accomplishes it.

No doubt, Beth probably thinks I'm going to flip around and snap the mother's neck.

"Trust me," I breathe out the side of my mouth. Beth helps me with my seatbelt in reply, deft fingers unleashing me in less than three seconds. Every muscle in me relaxes, because she passed an important test I hadn't realized I'd given.

Beth trusts me, even after everything I've put her and Essie through.

Now that the boa constrictor of a seatbelt is unlatched, I hitch my hips up slightly, hand delving deep into my pocket for a toy. Feeling around, because I never leave home without at least four of my favorites, I locate the purple, chubby cartoonish creature I've dubbed People Eater.

Turning in my seat, "Hey, little one," I coax softly, finding a red-faced, chubby toddler losing her shit. Blonde pigtails and a button nose, she can't be more than two, freaking out more because her mother is freaking out, than the flight itself scaring her.

"You're going to be okay, sweetheart," I croon, smiling and meaning it. "If your momma would relax, I know you would too," is a suggestion, but more of a threat to the woman who is glaring at me for interrupting her tirade on how little Ashlyn is a terrible child.

Ashlyn is a perfect child, whose mother is a stressed-out, over-emotional dingbat, who is making this worse for a flight filled with sleepy, yet equally stressed-out passengers.

"Squeeze this when you're scared." The chubby hand is already reaching for the foam People Eater– panic-stricken expression shifting instantaneously to glee, because Officer Devon is giving her a toy to play with, like her mother ought to have.

The toddler squeezes the toy, perfectly happy to rest against her momma and curl up, and hopefully take a long, *silent* nap.

The mother is seething, and little Ashlyn is no doubt still picking up on the vibe, thinking she's the cause. "You're too young to have kids– don't judge me."

Finger hitching across the aisle, "My oven– my bun." I show her the heart clenched in my hand. "Take it from someone who can feel how you're feeling... your daughter can too. The more upset you get, the worse she'll behave. If you want her to calm down, you need to do that first."

"Don't–"

"The entire plane is picking up on the vibe, lady," I warn, voice not unkind. "I used to be like your child, and my mother was a billion times more unsettled than you are, so listen to me, for the sake of your daughter when she's a grown woman. Calm yourself– you're asking something of a two-year-old, you've yet to learn yourself."

"Ashlyn always gets restless. I knew this would happen–" the mother's not hearing me, not realizing her stressing out over the anticipation of the girl freaking out is exactly what caused the girl to freak out in the first place, ear pain not included.

"You don't have to believe me, but you ought to take my advice. If you calm down, the flight will be a pleasant one for all of us. If it doesn't work, call me a liar when we deplane." Delving deep into my pocket, I pull out a foam strawberry, then hand it to the mother. "Play with this– you can keep it."

Turning back around in my seat, I ignore dozens of eyes on me, including those from the stunned flight attendant and Essie and Rory. Beth, I can't ignore her since she's sitting next to me, and she's business as usual, not surprised by my behavior in the least.

"I think that's why we get along so well," Beth starts speaking as if we've been holding a conversation for quite a while, which is usual for the pair of us. I know exactly what wasn't said, whereas the people around us probably think we're nuts.

"Before..." she trails off, because that's what everyone who's in the know says about me pre-nightmare. "You were highly intuitive back then, and I missed that Devon."

"He was always there," I remind Beth how I'm not a different person– I'll forever be me. "Just muted by drugs, because it was overpowering me. It's my greatest asset on the job, but also the reason why I fit my job too."

"True," Beth muses to herself, pitched in a singsong voice. "I'm glad we all have jobs that suit us, makes life more rewarding."

It's late, and Beth is a patient hunter, waiting me out. The plane settles into quiet silence, the lights above the seats going out, one by one, as the passengers turn in for a six-hour, overnight flight.

Shifting slightly, I'm thankful I'm small for a man– I fit in tighter spaces comfortably. Beth and I get cozy, both of us smiling fondly over how quickly Rory and Essie drifted off to sleep. Rory's arm is slung over Essie, Essie tucked tightly to his side, with her cheek pressed to his chest, palm curled beneath her chin. Rory's palm rests on our baby, cradling it protectively.

Peace settles over me, knowing it won't matter if I fail or succeed in protecting Essie, Rory and Beth will always have our backs. Essie and our baby will be protected, cared for– loved.

Tears sting my eyes, the relief so overpowering, I'm not sure how to release it to the world. Being me is stressful enough, the fear of fucking it all up is all-consuming. Where most husbands would get jealous of another man comforting their wife, I'm suddenly thankful. This world is hard enough for me to navigate when I'm just worrying about myself– adding Essie and our baby is exponentially more terrifying.

I want them– I need them. But I need support too, unable to give them everything they need and still have enough left to emotionally support myself.

"You'll be a good dad, Dev." Beth smiles at me, resting her hands in her lap over her big purse. "Not gonna lie... it was a shock to see you running around town, passing out parental advice."

Blushing, instead of looking away sheepishly, I stare Beth down in challenge. "I'm not passing out parental advice," I practically snarl. "I'm telling them how their kids feel."

"What do you mean?" is said in her coaxing, therapist voice.

"I know all about being the kid to bad parents," I grumble defensively. "They didn't know what they were doing. Dad was clueless. Mom was negligent and abusive, and she's not getting a mental illness pass on that. Even at my most rotten, I still didn't want to harm anyone."

"You feel close to the children," Beth muses, not a question– a statement. "So you champion for them."

"I'm twenty-one, and I know how lost I felt, even today... so these clueless, narcissistic parents piss me off. I can't stop myself."

"I worry about you–"

"No need." Snickering, I flash Beth a devious smirk. "At home, I approach them in my uniform. With my badge, they behave, even if I piss them off. I'll try to bite my tongue this weekend, but Rory's big body will deter someone from kicking my ass."

"You need to worry about us all now." Beth reaches over to lay her hand on top of where mine are clasping the foam heart. "You're the strongest person I know. All fortitude and will, and big balls, but not brute strength. Protect us all by protecting yourself. *Behave.*"

"Yes, Mom," I tease, but I'm hearing her.

"That's what I wanted to talk to you about," Bethany practically breathes, shifting to settle closer to me. Shoulders touching, heads turned toward one another, the quiet intimacy would normally have my tics triggered, but this is Beth.

"You and I need to come to an agreement," Beth negotiates. "I've already talked to Rory and Essie, so you don't need to unless you want to–"

"Of course, you have," I twist out nastily, hating how I'm the last person to find out what Beth wants.

"Behave," Beth chastises again, trying to get me in hand. "We both know Rory and Essie are followers– ain't no shame in that. So it's you and I who have to come to an agreement, and they will follow us anywhere."

We are on an overnight flight to Las Vegas, after all, proving how easily I can manipulate both Rory and Essie. "True," I whisper, leaning forward slightly to see around Beth.

Rory's chest is rising and falling in a peaceful rhythm, with Essie wiggling to find a more comfortable position.

It's wrong of me, but I call Essie my zealot. She has a mind of her own, and the voice to get what she wants, but when it comes to me, she'll give me anything I want. This is a fact no one will ever dispute.

Rory, on the other hand, he seems to tap into a place where he knows what's good for me, and will fight me if I'm asking to be enabled.

Then there's Beth– I ain't getting shit over on this woman. The last time I wigged out on her, she beat the living hell out of me, then hit me again when her fingernail broke. In her defense, Beth doesn't believe in violence, but we were both at our breaking point.

"What do you want to talk about?" I pretend my voice didn't warble, and my fingers aren't clenching and releasing the foam heart in my palm.

Beth's right. We're in charge.

"We could battle to the death," I tease, voice serious. "If you weren't around, they'd both be mine."

"Keep in mind…" Beth trails off, eyes flickering all over my body, no doubt thinking how she'd hand me my ass. "I'd win."

"I've been working out." I hitch my pantleg up, not bothering to hide my erection. "Better diet, exercise, meds, and no downers… it might be an even fight."

A front tooth sinks into Beth's bottom lip, as she struggles not to laugh too loudly for the silent flight. "Or, instead of fighting each other, we could just come to an agreement."

"Essie's mine," I snarl, knowing damned well Essie belongs to Bethany too. "I'll share, but you need to share Rory too. We'll just ignore how jealous we are."

Still struggling to stay silent, Beth's chest moves up and down rapidly as she fights her own laughter. A hand is thrust out for a shake. "Fair deal, Devon, since you're in love with my husband."

After three solid pumps, I release Beth's hand. "But the real question remains, are you in love with my wife?"

"Give me a minute," Beth rumbles, face twisted with indecision. "This isn't something I spoke about with either of them."

Satisfied I'm the first to know, I scooch back into my seat, tugging my pantleg down since my nuts were getting squished. Content to wait, I pocket the foam heart.

"I have no sexual hang-ups. My sexuality is as fluid as it gets." Bethany answers a question Rory and I have been debating for weeks. We all love to say we're open, but we're about as private as private gets, keeping shit real close to the vest. None of us had the balls to come out and just ask Beth.

"I love Essie," Beth admits without hesitation. "I'm physically attracted to her, just as much as you are, Dev– but I know Essie inside and out, and I know she's as straight as straight can get."

Our eyes flash to where Essie is resting on Rory, thinking how they're both each other's type. Essie and Beth, that ain't ever happening, even if it'd make shit easier on all of us.

"Yeah, but..." I trail off, having no idea how to say what I want to say, which is bizarre, since I'm known as the blunt one.

"I struggled before Rory came to me." Beth turns more toward me, crowding closer. "I'd love to say my hesitation was because of Auggie's agreement and the Playroom, but that's not true. I love Rory. I want Rory. I love being Rory's wife. I want to share a life with him. But–"

"But?" I coax, because Beth is clamming up on me, and that's not something I've ever seen before.

"You were made to wear the uniform– it's your nature. Your lack of nurturing has you empathizing with children. There would be no Primp without Essie. Rush flows in Rory's veins, more than it ever has Auggie and Robin's– maybe equally with Isis. What I want, what I'm good at, it's not just sitting in a chair while my patient rambles their problems."

"Been there, done that… just yesterday," I mutter wryly, knowing I'll probably have more hours receiving therapy than Beth will ever have giving therapy.

"Let's just say, I had more than one motive for pushing you and Rory together, and it doesn't take the gift I was giving you away, just because it also benefits me."

"Rory feels guilty as fuck," I remind Beth of the bitter truth. "We haven't fooled around much, just *hugging*."

"Your bond is emotional, sexual, and romantic, and I hoped that would help me explain my stance to Rory, even though mine is clinical in nature."

"You want to fuck your patients," I blurt out harshly, understanding Beth as well as she understands me.

"No," Beth stresses, eyes glaring at me in challenge. "This is what I was built to do, Devon. I want to help those in my office, but another grouping of people in the Playroom. You know better than most how a tragic sexual experience will chase you for life, erasing any happiness you find."

My mind flashes to Robin, how tightly he held me. Arms squeezing me tighter and tighter, until all I felt was safe, safe to touch myself. Safe to lose control enough to get off, because I trusted Robin to give me my control back once the euphoria was gone. It wasn't sexual for either one of us.

"See?" Beth reaches for my hands again, twining hers with mine, squeezing just as tightly as Robin had. "We all need different people in our lives to fulfill specific needs. No *one* person can be our be-all, end-all. Look at Clover and your dad, and how they survived the loss of a spouse."

Eyes closing, I never want to think about losing Essie, but I know if Essie lost me, she would be well taken care of by those who love her and me. That, in and of itself, is a comfort.

"Robin's been a big influence on me, just as my professors have been. I know I can help people, Devon." The squeezing gets tighter. "But Rory is so traditional, he would never understand without experiencing what it was like to have his loyalties divided. That guilt over needing you and wanting Essie will help him understand when I explain."

"You're going to fuck your patients," I mutter again, this time with less venom and more understanding. "Pre-Devon Rory would have never got it."

"There's a girl in my study group. I won't go into detail, but I know I can help her– I have the tools she needs to heal. What kind of person would I be to not help, just because it will upset my husband?"

"If Rory loves you, he'll understand. It's not cheating, Beth. I get it."

"Thank you." Beth's entire body slumps, relief palpable. "Thank you for being on my side– I'll need you to help me explain. I don't want to do this for my own pleasure, but for their healing. I can help, Dev– I know I can."

"What are we going to do, Bethany?" I beg, tears glistening in my eyes. "What are we going to do, because I feel the same fucking suffocating guilt too… how do I tell my wife I'm in love with your husband? How do I tell Rory, knowing it will hurt him too? What about our friends, and family… the town? What about our kids when they get older?"

"I feel so selfish," Bethany sobs, the mournful sound nearly silent. My arms part on instinct, cradling my best friend to my chest. "What a can of worms I've opened, eh? All because I wanted Rory to experience that same torn sensation that's killing me."

Chuckling without humor, I hug Bethany as we both silently cry. "We need a plan, and we need to stick to it. Why you did what you did doesn't matter. What we do in the aftermath does."

"Your therapy-speak gets me hot." Beth giggles softly against the side of my throat. "Totally inappropriate to say, but the truth nonetheless. I like how you and I can talk about things Essie and Rory will never understand."

"Our over-educated best friend is having a hard time dumbing herself down enough to talk to us simpletons?" I tease, understanding. "I get it– I thought my brain would bleed while you guys planned the reception at Rush."

"Mine too." Beth giggles again, voice lighter with her confession. "Rory felt weird just hanging out with Essie, because it was the two of them who were most excited, like he was cheating on us… or maybe it was too girly? I don't know."

"Our boy has a big problem with thinking masculinity is tied to anything but the fact he has a dick in his pants," I mutter sardonically. "I call Rory out on it nonstop. He's a social butterfly. Our party boy. The event planner. I'm glad he can do these things with Essie, because it's taxing for me to be *on* long enough to suffer through the party, let alone the planning of it."

"We complement each other in varying ways." Pulling away slightly, Bethany looks me straight in the eyes. "I've been studying facets of polyamory and its societal pitfalls, long before Rory came back into my life. After watching Auggie, Robin, and Isis fight it so hard, it made me curious. Then I discovered polyamory fit me– it felt right."

"I just learned what demisexual means, Beth– don't hit me with this bullshit and expect me to know what you're talking about. I may eat, sleep, breathe, and shit therapy-speak, but it's not sexual in nature. We stick to PTSD, bipolarism, addiction, and me being on the spectrum."

"Yeah, sorry." Blushing beautifully, Beth pulls away to sit firmly in her seat, but she leaves her palm resting on my side. "It's nice having someone understand."

"Just explain, then I will understand," I mutter patiently, figuring it must be hard to have that huge brain in her head, and have to hide it from us simple folks. Beth loves to act all bubbly and happy. But since I've been back, I've noticed how contemplative she is, watching more and more, instead of participating in our cheesy conversations.

"What's polyamory?" I ask, more so than curiosity getting the better of me, but because I can sense how badly Bethany wants me to be interested in things she doesn't discuss with anyone outside of her study groups.

"A relationship between more than two people," Beth mutters pointedly, eyes flashing to where our sleeping spouses are cuddled together. "It will take work, but I think it's a perfect fit for all four of us."

"Because Rory and I accidentally hooked up?" Guilt and shame slam into me, when I'd promised myself I'd stop the self-flagellation routine. I may have a substance addiction, which most of the time hides mental illness, but I seem to be more addicted to making myself bleed guilt. It's been a struggle to fight myself every step of the way.

"No, Devon." Beth's fingers clench into my t-shirt, pulling the fabric tight across my stomach. "Polyamory. Because I'm not built for monogamy– because I don't ever want to be monogamous, as if it's a gauge on fidelity, faithfulness, or love. Because I need to be able to touch my clients without feeling debilitating guilt. Because Rory's bisexual, and tried to smother that side of himself, and he wants you *and* Essie too. Because Essie needs things from Rory, things you can't give her, and we both know it… Most importantly, because you need a support system of people who complement you in all areas, and we want to be those people for you."

Swallowing down a sob of my own, I hold my eyes wide, and it's not panic or anxiety that is inundating me. A feeling of rightness descends, and I don't know what I did to deserve it. To deserve not one, but three people who will love me unconditionally.

"I think polyfidelity would be a perfect fit for us, with the exception of me in a clinical sense, where I will help my clients in the Playroom. While the pleasure will be physiologically impossible to ignore, that is just a means to an end. I will be faithful emotionally to all three of you, romantically to Rory, while you three are emotionally, sexually, and romantically faithful to each other. Essie and I will have a platonic, sisterly bond, and you and I…"

"I'm not in love with you, Beth," I admit, blurting it out harsher than I meant it to be. "I love you. I promise never to hurt you, to always be there for you. But I can't be in love with you too– *I can't*. I don't have any more of that type of love in me."

"We're too much alike, you and I." Beth fills in where I left off, knowing exactly how I feel, because she feels exactly the same way too. "But I want to fuck you." She's even blunter than I am sometimes.

Laughing in shock, my eyes go wide and my grin freezes into place. "Half the time, I'm so goddamn jealous of you, I don't know whether or not I want to murder you or fuck you into submission."

"Channel it into fucking." Beth's face blushes bright red, but not from embarrassment. *Arousal*. "I want you, not gonna lie. It would be like riding a wild bull or harnessing a storm, and I want to experience it, since I'm giving my husband to you and your wife."

It would be so easy to do as Bethany's asking. She truly is giving us Rory, at her own expense. Watching how close Rory has gotten to Essie, their friendship tighter than ever. It's not romantic or sexual, even though it's obvious they appreciate the other's outside packages– Rory and Essie do fit, and their friendship could so easily turn to more if the guilt was gone.

...if the guilt was gone.

That's the uphill battle to be fought by all of us– one I've been struggling against nonstop for too many weeks to count. The more time I spent with Rory, the more time Rory spent with Essie, the more time I spent around Bethany, the more I loved them all, in differing ways... the more I needed them near me. The more I struggled to fit us all together into a socially acceptable package where we didn't all get hurt in the process.

"It sounds like Rory's getting the best part of the deal, with all of us clamoring for his love and attention." Rolling over Beth's words, the hardest truth hits me out of nowhere. "You're being left out because Essie doesn't swing that way, and I can't fall in love with you... but the high cost is how you're the one who will have fun outside of our bedrooms."

"To *help* my clients, not for my own personal, sexual gratification," Beth stresses hard.

"I get it– I do." Palm lifting on its own accord, I find myself rubbing Beth's hand, where it rests against my side. "But will Rory and Essie?"

"They won't want to have an open relationship, Devon." Beth's expression shifts to total seriousness. "It's one of the reasons Rory and I wouldn't work in a sexually monogamous relationship. Always soft, when I need hard sometimes. They aren't built that way. They need the stability of a solid relationship with people who adore them, with partners who will cherish them. They need constant reassurance and validation, and going outside the relationship will murder their self-confidence and security... and you need that too, Devon. *You do*."

Stability is the cornerstone of my sanity, so I agree with Beth on that factor. "They won't understand your need to help people, using yourself as an example–"

"But you do, and I only need one of you to get it," Beth drives right over me. "What do you need?"

"The ability to negotiate different rules if things change," I blurt out without thought. "I can't be locked into rules, into promises I might not be able to keep. That will stress my ass out until I crash and burn. I need a failsafe, a ripcord, something that will let me know if I fail, you guys won't leave me."

"Oh, Devon," Beth cries out softly, arms reaching out to pull me into a hug. "Every day is a negotiation when you're in a relationship. If I've learned anything, it's that human beings were created to evolve, and it's being forced to remain in stasis that has so many in therapy."

"Don't I know it," I mutter wryly against Beth's cheek.

"Monogamy isn't for everyone, no matter how hard society tries to smash square pegs into round holes. On the flip side, polyamory doesn't mean you can't have a faithful relationship. Polyfidelity, with rules that can be negotiated and discussed however often need be."

"We're doing this?" I mutter in shock, eyes bright, sweat dampening my t-shirt. I've been freaking out, aching for them when I'm not around them, finally understanding Essie's bizarre need to have Beth shoved up her ass now that I feel the loss when Rory isn't sitting next to me.

I used to tease Essie, how she couldn't go five minutes without texting Beth. *I gotta tell Beth about this sale I just saw. I wanna talk about what just happened on the Bachelor. God, this cake was so good, I gotta tell Beth about it, so maybe she'll learn to make it for us. There's a new contouring video– I'm so excited!*

I thought Essie was nuts, totally codependent on her best friend, until I caught myself doing it too. Like how if my therapist said something truly profound, I'd call Beth from the parking lot after my session. Or a hot car would breeze by me, just hedging their bets with my radar gun, and I'd text Rory how I wanted to test-drive that type of car next. Or how I suddenly turned clingy, sending cat videos to Beth when I needed five seconds of attention, or a simple **HI** to Rory at random times during the day.

Because, Lord knows, I bug the piss out of Essie, and she needs some breathing room.

To have the ability to turn and tell Rory or Beth the stupidest of things that pops into my mind, like how comforting it is to know Essie's there to listen and roll her eyes at me. But, lately, I've felt off-kilter, more often texting the stupid bullshit to them, because they are off living their own lives, as if Essie and I aren't a pivotal part of it.

Now I wonder whether or not Rory and Beth have been feeling the same way. The guilt. The shame...

The empty ache.

"We're really doing this?" The relief is so palpable, it steals my breath away.

"Yeah," Beth whispers conspiratorially. "And now we need to think of something as an ice-breaker, because Rory and Essie are too skittish, too guilty–"

"Not ballsy and shameless like us," I add with a devious snicker.

"Exactly." Beth winks at me, grinning. "Once they have sex with each other, they'll get it."

Unconditional love means I don't get jealous, not even a fragment.

Essie will be with Rory before I've had a chance, and the jealousy tries its damnedest to rise, but is easily smothered. That's because I love them both, love us all enough to need it, to want it, to scheme to get it.

There's comfort in knowing I have a devious partner in crime, and Beth and I will easily switch who's in charge, depending on the situation. "Leave that up to me, and follow my lead."

CHAPTER THREE

After a hella long flight, the rush at the airport, and the bazillion people flooding into Las Vegas, we took an easy consensus on getting a hotel off the strip, for my sanity's sake. I don't do well at people-ing. Rory and Essie are sitting on a sofa, guarding our bags, because Essie's feet hurt due to the flight adding to her usual pregnancy issues. Beth and I are in charge, leaving Rory to sit with my wife.

Having more than two people in this relationship is helpful in the extreme, as I couldn't have been in two places at once. As much as I would have hated Essie being on her feet to stand in line next to me, no way in hell would I have left her alone in a strange hotel.

We find ourselves at a middle-of-the-road hotel chain, just off the strip. The upside is how we don't have to deal with flowing booze, casino traffic, high-rollers, or gaggles of obnoxious, drunken bachelor and bachelorette partiers. The downside is how families seem to be staying here.

There are a ton of kids outside of their normal routines, with parents who don't seem to get how that's disruptive to their tiny nervous systems. Whether the kids are on the spectrum or not, the parents don't seem to get how the kids need a mental, emotional, and physical time-out while traveling, and not in the punishment sense of the word. If the parent is burnt out, the kid needed to decompress hours ago.

Beth keeps sighing and rolling her eyes, as if she's wired directly into my head, listening to my internal chattering. We share a wry look as we finally step up to the front desk.

"Just you and the missus?" A perky, middle-age woman smiles at us, fingers clacking away. "Honeymooning, are you? Would you like a king?"

"We would *love* a king." My lips curl into a devious smirk, and Beth freezes next to me, sensing I'm about to unleash my inner asshole.

At the airport, some douchebag called me a faggot for leaning against Rory during the tram ride. Since, Rory's avoided touching me, not necessarily to avoid being bashed, but fearing me retaliating.

"Just me and the missus." I repeat the front desk lady's words back to her, while hitching my finger over my shoulder toward the sofa where Rory and Essie are sitting, then I point to Beth. "And her and her mister too."

"Excuse me?" Confused, synapses shorting out, the lady shakes her head slightly.

"It's our honeymoon." I smile sweetly, turning on the Mason charm. "We'd love a king-sized bed... and it will be the four of us. Thank you."

Sliding my credit card and driver's license across the counter, I never break my gaze from the front desk lady's. No doubt she's seen worse– we are in Las Vegas, after all. But it's seeing four fresh-faced *kids*, one with a bun in the oven, that's confusing the piss out of her.

After I get through the usual rigmarole, keycards in hand, Beth and I fight our smirks as we make our way back to Rory and Essie. I grab a few bags, shouldering them.

"Everything good?" Rory stands, rubbing his sweaty palms on his thighs, while licking his dry lips to dampen them.

"Just dandy," I mutter absentmindedly, passing out the keycards, causing Beth to crack up slightly. "Lady was real nice to us." With one eye on Beth, who's having a time of it, I reach to help Essie stand from the sofa.

"This baby." Essie struggles, reaching backward to prop herself upward. "I'm not that far along– not gonna survive the last of my third trimester, if I'm this big during the second."

"You're a dinky person, Ess." Beth reaches out to help me, because I'm not that big either. Plus, I'm already loaded down like a pack mule with the bags. "But I fear you have a Mason growing in your belly."

"Mason!" I point at myself, gesturing all over the place, causing Rory to bust a gut.

"Mason," Beth states pointblank. "As in Malcolm, Ren, and Weston sized... you inherited your mother's size."

"I'll have you know—" I reach for my wife's hand, clutching it firmly in mine as we head for the elevator bank. "The Jamisons are not small people— look at Aunt Ginny. My mom was also a big woman. My granddad, Berry, he was a husky fella too, always failing his physical fitness tests."

"Well," Beth sighs, striding forward to walk next to me. "When you finally have a girl, she may be a voluptuous woman, probably short though. *Like you*," she teases me, poking me in the spine.

"Will's gonna be Mason-sized." Rory's long reach manages to rub the back of my neck, when he's walking on the other side of Essie from me. "But that's why Ess is so big already. Tiny frame, big baby, makes her look even bigger."

"Ugh! Thanks," Essie mutters grumpily, stepping inside the elevator. "Rub it in, why don't ya?"

"As much as I'd love my son to look like my dad, he's destined to be a tiny shit— yet another trait he'll wish he didn't inherit from me."

"We need naps," Rory tries to redirect my emotions, before I start listing off how my genes are flawed.

"And food," with Beth joining the fray.

"And massages," Essie says pointedly in my direction, raising an eyebrow, just asking me to disagree.

"And privacy," I add as we step off the elevator. "I can't people for a few hours, or else I'll go on a fucking rampage on the next parental figure I spot." My words are loud, and hit their intended target— the frustrated couple trying to wrangle their kids onto the elevator we just evacuated.

"Naps," we all mutter in unison, sanity winning out, as I open up the door to our room, using the keycard.

The honeymoon suite welcomes us. With the bedroom separated from a large sitting area and mini-kitchen by a half wall, with a bathroom promising a larger bathtub and shower stall. The décor is the usual fare, nothing special, but clean and neat.

"What the...?" comes from Rory and Essie, and Beth finally releases the laughter she'd been swallowing. "Is this... is this the honeymoon suite?" Essie's confused, but it's Rory who has me finally losing it.

"A king-sized bed?" Marveling, Rory stares down at the mattress in wonder. "But... how? Why?"

Dropping the bags to the floor with an audible thump, I'm highly entertained by Essie and Rory trying to figure out why there is only one bed, to the background soundtrack of Beth giggling sadistically.

After waiting for more than twelve hours, I do what I've wanted to do again since the restroom at Rush... I kiss the motherfucking hell outta Rory, leaving him a breathless puddle slumping to the bed.

"I feel better now... about that nap?" I hightail it to the bathroom, needing a moment to myself. "I get first dibs on the potty. In two hours, I'll need some food for my meds," I warn how our naps will be short-lived.

It's a little past ten a.m., after taking an overnight flight, getting through the airport, arriving at the hotel to check in, and we haven't slept or ate since yesterday morning, except for a few interrupted winks on the flight. I knew today would be about acclimating and just being together, with tomorrow exploring what Las Vegas has to offer.

*_*_*

Curled up on the outside of the king-sized bed, Beth is softly snoring, zonked out because we spent the flight planning our future and scheming how we were going to get it. Rory's eclipsing all sight of Beth, lying on his side, facing Essie and me. On the outside, I'm rubbing Essie's lower back and hips, while she rests on her side, facing Rory.

"What should we do today?" Rory isn't tired one bit, and neither is Essie, not after sleeping through the entire flight. "We gambled last time, but..." he trails off, fearing there are too many triggers in Sin City for me.

"Unless there's a huge group of addicts toking up a bowl, or filling a syringe, and then passing it around at the roulette table, I'm good. Alcohol isn't a problem for me." I reach over Essie to squeeze Rory's shoulder. "Have a drink– don't go without on my behalf. My not imbibing is twofold. Drinking isn't my addiction.

It's an addictive substance, but it's how it interferes with my meds that's the real issue."

"I don't need it to have fun…" Rory trails off, looking sheepish. "But once in a while, I'm going to want a drink or two."

"Don't feel guilty." This time it's Essie who reaches out to Rory, comforting him with her touch. "Once I have the baby, I'm going to have a glass of wine once in a blue moon, but not around Devon for a while."

"The more you drink around me–" I pull Essie's back to my chest, wrapping my arms around her, between her belly and tits, then I rest my chin on her shoulder, so I can talk directly to Rory. "It won't make me want to drink– more like desensitize me to it. So have a beer if you wanna. It's drugs that are my driving force."

I don't want people to avoid me because they see me as broken, or like I'm the teetotaler police who is not-so silently judging like Willow loves to do. It would just make me feel more abnormal, and feed into my need to bleed guilt.

If this is going to work between us, I'm not going to change who they are. I know Rory smokes with Robin, and I'm good with that as long as it's not around me. My resolve isn't strong enough to witness it… not when it's the smell that trips the triggers in my brain.

"I'm up for some gambling this afternoon, while the rowdy crowd is still in bed." The less people, the better for me.

Chuckling to myself, Peggy Webster pops into my head. When I was a little kid, my grandparents and the Websters took a trip to Las Vegas, and all Peggy could talk about was the all-you-can-eat buffets, and not in a good way. Being big people, Berry and Maeve Jamison loved the buffets.

"We need to hit a buffet," I mutter jokingly, but judging by the glazed expressions on Essie and Rory's faces, they think I'm being serious.

"I could eat," Rory mutters in agreement. "I could always eat."

"I'm eating for two," Essie says in the same dreamy tone. "I'm hungry nonstop."

"Cake," Beth breathes out in her sleep, picking up part of our conversation in her dreams.

"At least they have salad," I contribute, always finding eating a tedious affair. "I'm not trusting fish this far from a seaboard."

"I'm too keyed up, but Beth needs sleep." Sheepishly giddy, Rory's practically vibrating to get out and find adventure.

"My body may be uncomfortable, but my mind won't shut off," Essie mutters in agreement.

"Welcome to my world," I tease, hoping they realize that unsettled sensation is just a fragment of what I feel every given second of my life. "I have an idea…" I trail off, brain doing its checks and balances, weighing the pros and cons. "How about you and I give Essie a nice massage to make her feel better while Beth sleeps, then we'll all be ready to go take Sin City by the balls?"

"Are you sure?" Essie and Rory gulp in unison, and I don't blame them one bit.

Out of everyone, the people in this bed know I'm not a changed man. I'm still me, a jealous, vindictive, plotting asswipe. When I catch Rory or Essie giving the other an appreciative look, I find it amusing, because I know exactly what they are appreciating and why. When I catch Rory or Essie giving anyone else a look, a red wash of possession fills my vision.

It's for that very reason I begged Beth not to connect with me too closely, because she would be losing both her hands for touching her clients, no matter her altruistic reason. It's not that I have no more love to give– it's that it's stressful enough to worry about Rory and Essie nonstop, that I can't add Beth to the list. There can be no romantic love between Beth and me, because Rory and Essie will eventually understand Beth's need for practical, hands-on therapy, whereas my possessive side would stop her… and that would harm us all.

It's a good thing Essie and Rory are so loyal. They may get lusty thoughts, but they'd never act on them, never *want* to act on them, and that's why we're all a good fit.

I never realized I didn't think like everyone else, assuming my sexuality was fucked due to the nightmare. But, as I've healed, I've witnessed firsthand how Rory, Essie, and Beth check people out, getting a flushed look of arousal about them. When

I've only ever looked at people and thought, *she's pretty or he's handsome*, with no sexual bent to the thought, whatsoever.

I've come to realize no one on the planet thinks as I do.

Instead of explaining, my fingers begin unbuttoning Essie's dress. I'm no fashionista, so I have no idea what this dress is called, but the dress looks like a long blouse, buttons all the way to the hem. Handy for us, comfortable for Essie, yet equally enticing. Since she changed into the cotton dress, I've contemplated unsnapping all those buttons.

One thing that I do ask of Essie, if she's anywhere near me, where we'll be touching, is specific fabrics are no-go for me. Only the thinnest of denim. Corduroy is actually fun for me to touch, finding the grooves interesting. Satin or silk is nice, but when it snags on a hangnail, I flip the fuck out. Yarn is absolute torture. Soft cuddly blankets, made of chenille or microfiber, but I have to do a touch-test first– hangnails again. Jersey cotton is my absolute favorite. Thankfully, most of the stuff Essie owns is made of cotton anyway.

It's why Rory will continually receive gifts, until his wardrobe is Devon-friendly. I hate button and zipper waistbands, and just looking at them on Rory skeeves me out.

Socks. Paper. Styrofoam. Talc. Yarn. Wool. If I could, I'd eradicate those substances from the planet. If I come into contact with any of them, I immediately have to put on hand lotion.

Soft, creamy skin, that's the perfect antidote. "Mmm…" I murmur, hands slipping the two halves of Essie's dress apart, exposing her bra and panties. Smile curling, I'm entertained with how Rory is pretending to look at Essie's belly, his eyes heavy lidded, when he's actually watching Essie's nipples harden through her thin, cotton bra.

This is step one in Operation Polyamory.

Beth *is* sleeping, but this scenario was prearranged on the flight here.

"That feel good?" I murmur softly into Essie's ear, eyes watching every muscle twitch in Rory's body. "Hmm?" fingertips trailing over her tits, I swirl around her hardened nipples. "Maybe Rory could help me, yeah?"

Wearing a drugged expression, Rory doesn't stop me as I press both of his hands directly over Essie's tits, squeezing slightly before I let go. It takes everything in me not to chuckle at their reactions. Essie jolts, like she's hooked up to a livewire, while Rory kind of slumps forward in shock.

"The world's most gorgeous tits," I whisper in appreciation, knowing Essie has a hang-up about them, thinking big tits make her a whore.

Beth and I had worried this would trip those negative triggers, but it's Rory. Rory's been our friend since we were in preschool. Rory's had our backs, been in love with Beth for as long as we can remember, and has looked at Essie like she's his own personal cupcake. They flirt, and they appreciate, now they can touch too, and Beth and I are good with that.

Rory's not an asshole frat brother looking to get off, not giving two shits whether she wants him or not– Rory cares about Essie, and only wants to touch her to make them both feel good.

Anyone else, I'd cut their goddamn hands off.

"Yeah… that's nice," I breathe in a coaxing, soothing tone, as my fingers expertly flick the clasp on Essie's bra.

The satisfied chuckle is impossible to smother as I witness Rory losing his shit. Jaw unhinging, mouth open wide, he makes a grunting, grumbling sound of awe. I'm pretty sure there's drool on his lower lip.

Essie's terrified over how big her belly is, fearing stretchmarks, thinking I won't find her sexy anymore. If anything, pregnancy has made her even more beautiful. As I said, I'm from a long line of voluptuous women. My grandma and mom and aunt were all plus-sized, and Isis is no tiny waif of a woman. Beth's not small either.

Essie will forever be a dinky person– curvy in all the right places, but naturally petite. So it's a treat to see her pregnant.

As Rory touches her, the confidence I can't seem to give Essie fills her eyes and adds a pink flush to her skin.

We've discussed this– Beth and I –how Essie needs validation I can't seem to give her. Essie knows I love her unconditionally, thinking I'll lie to make her feel good about herself. But Rory isn't me. He's a virile man whose cock gets hard whenever he's aroused, and it's an obvious hard-on in loose cotton pants.

Essie needs what I cannot give her– no amount of therapy will change what's intrinsically Essie –and I'm selfless enough to make sure she gets it from someone we both love and trust.

Making purring, content sounds in the back of my throat, my fingertips glide over Essie's belly, dipping beneath the waistband of her panties. Sinking further, my fingers slip between slick, hairless folds, finding a tight bud begging for attention.

Moaning, Essie arches back into me, breath hitching in her throat, as Rory manipulates her tits and I rub swirls around her clit.

Ignoring the ache in my crotch, I have to continually tell myself this is step one of a two-step process, and I need to back away smoothly and let nature take its course. This isn't about me, and if I come now, I won't be able to function again until sometime tomorrow morning.

Me having a hard-on is a big fucking deal for Essie. I'll be able to participate, but not truly join in the fun if I accidentally pop off right now.

"Mmm… Rory needs some attention too," I breathe in a rhythmic tone. "Do you know what takes the edge off, keeps those swarming bees from flying around in your head?" One palm rubbing between Essie's thighs, I struggle to reach out to Rory. "Getting off."

Arm sliding between Essie and along the mattress, I tug the front of Rory's pants down, knowing damned well he's going commando. Rory's wood is pressed tightly to his belly, cockhead dark purple and beaded with precum.

Curling my toes against the need to join in and get off with them both, by living out a fantasy in reality, I'm patient instead.

"Feels so nice, doesn't it?" I purr into Essie's ear while slipping my hand from inside her panties, fingers sticky with her juices. Ever so slowly, I skate my fingertips along her arm, stopping at her wrist. Then I take control of Essie's hand, pressing her fingers around Rory's impressive girth.

On contact, they both moan in unison, a guttural sound that travels like a swift kick straight to my junk. Gritting my teeth, I try to control my need to shoot.

Essie's a fast learner, doing exactly as I showed her, and nothing else.

This time, I run my fingertips along Rory's arm, leaving one of his hands behind on Essie's tit, while I commandeer the other to dip into her saturated panties. With them mutually masturbating each other, I turn over onto my side, away from them.

"Have fun!" I mutter in a groggy tone, hand shoved down my own pants, fist clenching my junk punishingly, to stop myself from popping off. "I'm going to get that nap in now, while Beth's asleep. Enjoy yourselves– now you won't be bored while we catch a few winks."

Grinning, punishing my sack, I know Rory and Essie won't deviate from where I placed their hands, but they didn't say no and they sure as shit don't look guilty. The moans are breathy and soft, like they're making sure not to wake Beth and me, when there's no way I can sleep through this.

This step in our journey isn't about Beth or me. We know what we want, and we know how Essie and Rory feel about us. It was Rory and Essie who needed to explore the limits of their connection, before we can go a step further.

Step 2 of Operation Polyamory will be tonight, in this very room.

CHAPTER FOUR

"This is exactly what I needed." Slumping deep into the hot tub, with Essie sitting on the lip with her legs in the water. "I love seeing all the different shit, but in small intervals." I tug Essie's leg across my chest, then begin attacking the arch of her foot with my fingertips. Her moans are swallowed by the hot tub motor giving us bubbles.

"We need a hot tub." Of all people, I'm shocked it's Rory who voiced that.

"Aunt Ginny has one," I mutter arrogantly, loving how I've been in it many a time.

"Bet you wished Nurse Opal was still my puppy handler." Beth has us all choking on our tongues. "We should see if we could install one on the upper deck we share with the big apartment."

"Ain't sharing shit with Auggie– he needs to get his ass home," Rory grumbles, alerting the couple nearest to us. There's a few couples in the gigantic hot tub with us, but they've kept to themselves, so it hasn't pitched my anxiety too high. "If we make Auggie too comfy, he'll never leave."

"At least Isis is living at the Spook House now."

"I wonder–"

"Don't!" Comes from all directions, but it's Essie's tiny hand holding my mouth shut. Chuckling against Essie's palm, I lick her salty skin.

Auggie's intervention is a no-no topic on our mini-honeymoon, even though I know we're all thinking about it. Sneaky snake Beth, I bet she's called or texted while pretending to use the bathroom.

After our nap, where I didn't get a lick of sleep, because I was too keyed up after hearing Rory and Essie get each other off, but it was the lingering, addictive scent of sex that had me struggling the most, we hit the town. First stop was a buffet, where we took a shit-ton of selfies of how much my three best friends could hog down. I stuck to cooked vegetables, not trusting the fresh ones were washed properly.

We gambled for a bit, but they all assumed I'd be a Debbie Downer, because alcohol was flowing, drunks were gambling, pills were being popped, bachelorettes were driving me fucking nuts, and the bachelors kept looking at Essie's tits, even though she's pregnant. Then there was the fact that it was gambling, when I'm a money miser.

Needless to say, we cut the gambling short, because of their issue of assuming I wasn't having a good time, when I was. I won fifty bucks, so there is that.

After roaming around, people-watching while the girls hit a few shops, we made our way back to the hotel. Beth and I conspired, thinking the pool area would be a good aphrodisiac.

Foreplay for step two in Operation Polyamory.

"The Shithole doesn't have room enough for a dog house, let alone a hot tub," I mutter grumpily, as more people flood the pool area.

It was all adults in here, being conscientious. We've all spoken softly, while lounging in the hot tub as the others floated in the pool. Even the playful couples kept their enthusiasm down to a minimum.

We're here to relax, to have fun, and not be inundated by assholes who think the world revolves around them. It's been nice, until two grown women with a ton of kids invaded the area... and it's not the kids who are being obnoxious.

I do my best to fall back into our light, teasing conversation, ignoring how my ears are ringing and my skin is starting to tighten with anxiety.

"I don't mind Willow and Ren living with us," Essie says from above me, having to talk louder to be heard over the sound of the newcomers, just as every single person in the pool area has to do.

I pretend I don't see the women dragging chairs where they want them, when there were folded towels, bathing suit coverups, keycards, wallets, and cellphones resting in the seats.

The guy camping out in the corner of the hot tub lunges out to catch his shit before it falls into the pool, as the entitled cunt drags his chair away. Oblivious, the women only do and see what they want, as their children cannonball into the pool, upsetting and sinking several women who were floating on their backs.

"Hey, hold up a minute!" Watching as the guy hectically grabs for his shit, I do my best to ignore it.

Another couple dives to catch the poor guy's Kindle Fire before it falls into the pool, all the while the woman pretends nothing's happening around her. "Watch what the hell you're doing, lady!" The guy in the pool calls out, holding the Kindle high above the water to keep it safe.

The kids flood out of the pool, only to cannonball back in a second later, casting water high enough to spray the ceiling, and the Kindle is splashed from all sides, no matter how high the hero tries to raise it in the air.

…and just like that, the mood in the area shifts from peaceful to chaotic, and I siphon it from all directions.

Keyed to me, Rory's hand seeks out my thigh, beneath the water. Even in Sin City, Rory's been reluctant to touch me in plain sight. I'd worry he was embarrassed by me, or didn't want me, but he's protecting me from myself.

"I like living in a house filled with people," I mutter lightheartedly, still desperately trying to ignore the asshole women and their children. "It's all I've ever known. I'd be lonely otherwise."

"Only child!" Rory, Beth, and Essie mock shout, then giggle, "Jinx!"

"I get it." Essie begins rubbing my shoulders, fingers digging in nice and deep. "The Prynnes have a clan mentality too, so I was never truly alone. Ren and Willow can be a bit overwhelming though."

Chuckling, I remember how Ren yelled at Essie after moving-day, chastising her for only dreaming of sitting in a hot tub when pregnant. Ren can be a know-it-all puke sometimes, talking down to Essie, and not even realizing it. We had a good laugh about it, as Essie sat on the lip of the hot tub with her feet in the water, pouting because she couldn't get in with us. We promised to swim in the pool with her after we decompressed.

Decompressing ain't gonna happen now.

"Did you look up any shows?" I turn to Beth, trying my damnedest to not get involved in the chaos swirling around us. "We could go late tonight, or hit something tomorrow night... and honest, I'm good with gambling for a few hours at a clip. Not made of spun sugar."

"Cirque du Soleil tickets were available for tomorrow night, not too late either, since we'll want to get rested up for our flight home on Monday morning."

"We just got here this morning– let's not worry about going home already." Rory's mood has shifted, the worse the people act around us. What was supposed to relax us, to be foreplay, since we can't drink to lose our inhibitions, has actually backfired and turned us all ornery.

We're being held hostage in the pool area by self-involved assholes and their children. All attention is centered on the ruckus– it's like being in a tsunami with the noise-level and the amount of water pelting down around us. The hot tub is filled with our four-some and a few couples minding their own business in the opposing corners. The pool has a good dozen adults waiting patiently for the kids to tire out so they can get in a swim safely. Then there are the poor bastards who just want to sit in here and relax with their Kindles.

Fuck road-rage, I'm about to enter pool-rage territory.

"I have some mattress acrobatics planned tonight too," I croon with a wink to Essie, trying to play off Beth bringing up Cirque, but it falls like a dud.

"Alana!" The mother's voice cuts through the shrill screaming from the pool, both loud enough to shatter glass. "Alana! Alana, stop yelling!!!" Every eye in the hot tub flicks in my direction, waiting for me to blow like an overheating nuclear reactor.

Nerves vibrating, the last thread of my patience is about to snap. There is no amount of meds on this planet that can save me from this type of overstimulation.

I'm not concerned with the adults, as we can get up and walk our asses out of here. Maybe even hit up management to remove the disruption. It's the children I worry about, as they have no autonomy, forced to suffer through an auditory assault by their attention-seeking mothers.

Remember in little school, how a kid would be loud and obnoxious, begging for attention, but it always backfired. He'd get bullied, which was a shitty thing to do, but generally his bullies just wanted him to leave them the hell alone in the first place. He'd brag, all arrogance and zero confidence, almost delusional in his self-reflection. He'd never get any friends, because he was so fucking obnoxious, you'd rather avoid him than befriend him… as an adult lording over the school, I take it upon myself to tell this type of kid to slow their roll and calm down, and just be real. Their parents ignore them, so they over-compensate, which creates the monster who can't get friends. I don't hold back– I tell those kids the truth, they take my advice to heart, and they now have friends who like the real them.

These women are the grown-up versions of that kid, never learning no one wants to be near someone who is choreographing every movement and word out of their mouths, for optimum attention-gathering. They talk loudly, with over-exaggerated movements, anything to catch your attention, then suck it up, thinking they are hot shit and you can't look away, when all you want to do is literally drown them in the pool to regain sanity.

I don't need Beth's schooling to see they are creating another generation of children who are attention-starved, obnoxious assholes, who will in turn do the same to their children. The irony is how if the adults needed attention so badly, they ought to get it from their children, and then the children would get the attention they so badly need.

The mother has a cellphone fused to her hands, eyes never leaving the screen, as she sits all the way on the other side of the indoor pool area, the bubbling hot tub between her and her precious, precocious spawn. Her sister or sister-in-law– seems like the dudes in the family like a specific kind of worthless human being to breed their children– is chattering obscenely loud about how her husband never gives her a lick of attention, going as far as to insult his manhood with his children in earshot. Great mom, not realizing how bashing their father is cutting her sons' balls off before they even drop.

Six kids between them, all screaming like banshees, and most way old enough to know better, with a toddler's head bobbing precariously in the deep-end of the pool– one mother is too busy being a narcissistic bitch and the other is having an affair with whomever she's texting.

"Don't do it," Bethany warns, knowing the direction of my thoughts. Her eyes narrow, knowing me better in some ways than Essie or Rory. "Behave, Devon," she warns in the very tone those wastes of space should be using on their children. Calm. Firm. Authoritative.

"Alana!" The woman screeches, shrill voice causing my ears to ring. Every nerve in my body is poised for fight or flight, and we all know I'm not a coward. Stupid and brave, as Robin loves to call me, but never a coward. "Can you believe her?" The mother turns to her clone, totally exasperated by how her child is misbehaving. "I don't know what to do with them."

Mouth opening to tell the bitch exactly what she should be doing, Rory beats me to the punch. "What would you do, Dev?" Smiling slyly, he reaches over to rub Essie's baby bump, giving both my wife and our baby unconditional love and affection. "Since you have one of your own on the way."

"Alana!"

"What?" comes from four sources within the pool.

"Answer when I call you!" she yells across the pool area, alerting every person in a block radius. "Stop. Yelling." she enunciates slowly, yet louder than Alana could ever sound, as if the kid didn't know exactly what her mother's issue was in the first place.

"First thing I'd do–"

"Marco!"

Ducking, I experience a full-blown PTSD moment as precious Alana screams louder than before, in a power struggle with her childlike mother. "Was to not yell across the fucking pool, to tell my children not to yell in the fucking pool." I seethe, teeth clenched. "Then, if I told my kid no, and they didn't listen, I'd yank the little puke out of the pool and shove them ass-first on the tile for a long sit-in. If they did it again after their time-out, every-fucking-one of us would go back to our hotel room."

"What would that accomplish?" Bethany looks at me, head cocked to the side, curious, as if she's writing a case study on my ass.

"First, the kid would learn boundaries. Second, the world doesn't revolve around me. I wouldn't ruin the relaxation and fun of the twenty-some strangers in the pool areas, all because I'm a shitty parent, doing my damnedest to raise my children into assholes. Third, every one of those kids would gang up on the asshole because their fun was cut short. Trust me, pissed siblings and cousins are a billion times worse than a parent, because we hit and freeze out, and make their life miserable."

Bethany grins at me, while Rory reaches over to grab the back of my neck in a precursor to a kiss. Thinking the better of it, he leans back against the hot tub wall. It has nothing to do with morality– just fearing how I will answer questions when asked.

"I knew you were the right man to father my kids." Essie smiles blindingly in my direction. Instinctive, I do exactly what Rory wanted to do to me, only I do it to my wife. After a good thirty-second long kiss, I pull back, feeling more flushed than from the steaming hot water.

"If I remember correctly," I murmur, a devious smile splitting my lips, "I didn't exactly give you a choice in the matter."

Our laughter is cut short by a man bellowing, "Sandwiches!" from the doorway across the space, like it's a motherfucking picnic in their backyard, not the indoor pool area at a hotel with many other paying guests who don't give two shits about what they have to say or eat.

After dragging another chair, at least this one was belongings-free, the guy sits next to the texter and the gossiper, who I guess to be the texter's husband, since the gossiper says her husband is a no-show and a bunch of other unsavory insults. He puts a bunch of cellophaned sandwiches in their laps, then screams at the top of his lungs.

"Alana! Ethan! Kody! Greg! Sara! Finn!" voice breaking with the force, the bastard has my ears ringing so violently the blood in my veins boils. Before anyone can stop me, I'm to my feet, hopping out of the hot tub, and charging in their direction, trailing dripping water after me.

"Shut. The. Fuck. UP!" bellowing so loudly, my tonsils vibrate, I lean down into all three of their faces. "How do you like getting yelled at?" Clapping reverberates from around the enclosed area, mixed in with the blissful silence from the pool and the labored breathing of the three world's worst parents.

"You have no right–"

"Shut up," I warn, hand ready to cover the texter's mouth.

"You don't have kids," the gossiper tries to interrupt.

"Got one in there," I point to Essie and her obvious baby bump. "Raised my well-behaved siblings, I did. But that's not my issue– I'm thinking like a kid, like the rest of us being held hostage by your shitty behavior, not as a parent right now… Kids are meant to play, but not at the expense of terrorizing everyone else."

"Grow up," the gossiper snarls. "Just swim around them– ignore 'em like we do."

"My wife can't go into the pool like she's wanted to all night, because your precious angels would drown her with their cannonballs and splashing." Pointing upward at the droplets raining down on us, "Look at the goddamn ceiling and get a clue– you ruined that guy's Kindle, and nearly drowned all of his stuff when you stole his chair."

"Don't talk to my wife like that," the gutless, nutless wonder warns, teeth bared. The man is so fluffy, I could skip out of here and he wouldn't catch me while running.

"I don't need to be a parent to know you don't feed your children– *in the pool*," I stress. "I ought to take sister's cellphone and pitch it into the pool, then she'd finally pay attention to what was going on in there."

Mouth gaping open, the texter looks at her phone with guilt blazing in her eyes.

"Alana isn't little Finn's mother, and she shouldn't have to be a toddler's lifeguard. He was choking up water in the deep-end a few minutes ago." Pointing at the sign, "There's a reason there is no screaming, running, cannonballs, and eating in this place. No kids under fourteen without parental observation. *You* and your kids have yelled so much, we wouldn't notice if they were calling for help, when one of them is drowning after cramping up from eating the fucking sandwiches you shoved in their gullets."

"That's an old wives' tale–"

"No, it's really not," I mutter dryly. "Do you really want to know why your kids ignore you as you shout their names?" Dumbstruck, all three of them stare at me, while I hold their children's avid attention.

"First, because all you do is yell, and they're desensitized to it– you're doing exactly what you want them to stop. Second, because you ignore them. They came up to you, asking for attention– asking for you to watch them do flips and handstands, and you ignored them in order to bitch about him–" I point at the guy, realizing I got it wrong, and the wife is an ungrateful bitch, because clearly he's at least *present* in their lives. "Not only did every person in the area hear it, his *children* heard every emasculating word you said about him. Imagine what that will do to your sons? How it will teach your daughters to treat men?"

Head flipping around like the exorcist, "You were bitching about me?" The guy clearly doesn't realize what a waste of space he is married to.

"Yeah," I murmur smugly. "And she said you suck in the sack, and not in the good way." Ignoring how the guy is bubbling up for an epic bitch-fest, "Here's a novel idea… if you don't want your kids to yell, how about you stop yelling at your kids? Get off your lazy ass and actually go to your kid and make them listen. Stop playing the victim. Your kids weren't born assholes– you made 'em that way."

"Don't talk about my kids–"

"I like your kids, since they're just being kids." Leaning down, I get into all three of their faces, "I pity them for having you guys as their parents. You are your own worst enemy, and we shouldn't have to suffer in your presence, and your children will suffer as adults when they can't keep a job and have no friends and raise their kids by yelling, ignoring, and complaining about how bad their kids are."

Brushing my hands together, my job is done here. "Officer Devon says no more yelling, kids," I warn in a calm voice as I make my way back to the hot tub. I have all six of the kids' attention, and they mysteriously turn into actual angelic little shits worthy of love and attention. "If you're quiet, Rory and I will show you some fun pool games." *...since your parents are too fucking lazy and self-involved to do it.*

"Sorry. Not sorry for not behaving by keeping my trap shut." Slipping back into the hot tub, I close my eyes due to the energy in the pool area changing, not because of the calming effects of hot water. It's almost as if everyone can finally take a deep breath, and to think those kids live under that chaotic pressure every waking moment since their births.

"Weak people shouldn't breed together– someone has to take charge, and not all of us are cut out for it."

Eyes cracking open, Beth and I connect, knowing exactly who's in charge in this hot tub. Rory and Essie aren't weak in the manner in which I'm speaking. Spineless, lazy, and deluded is weak, not being submissive, kind, and caring. Rory and Essie will make incredible parents who will soothe our children after Bethany and I educate them.

CHAPTER FIVE

Sopping wet, and dripping our way back into our room, we're not as frustrated as we were, after playing with a pool full of kids and *big* kids too. The dad stopped licking his wounds, decided it was better to play with his kids, versus sit and listen to his wife and sister bitching up a storm. A few minutes into it, we both realized the other was a good dude, and got along famously.

"Dev, you can't–" Rory's unsure what kind of reception his chastisement will get, and it worries me how he's scared to speak his piece. "You can't go around doing what you just did in the pool."

"Yes, I can… and yes, I will." Calm, firm, and slightly amused, "I gave that guy his balls back, and his kids and wife will thank me for it."

Essie starts rooting around in our bags, knowing better than to challenge me on this topic, since we've had this conversation a dozen times in the past month alone. Beth's leaning against the wall, pretending not to be amused, since she's jacked up to what's playing out in my mind… or maybe both girls find Rory and me arguing as entertaining.

"Not every situation is dominance and submission, like in the Playroom." Rory folds his arms over his chest, eyebrows lowered in indignation. The man loathes the Playroom, not understanding it, and I know the conversation he's going to eventually have with Beth isn't going to end well.

"Actually…" I trail off, leaning down to grab a swath of blue cloth from the bag Essie's rooting around in. "It's you who makes the Playroom about sex. Dominant and submissive are core personality traits. For a submissive person put into a position of authority, *such as a parent*," I stress, "It's a comfort, the release of stress, to have someone who knows what they are doing as your partner. It's a balance– it's all a balance."

Eyeing Beth, we take three seconds to have a silent conversation, then I turn back to my wife. "We're gonna shower up together." Smiling slyly, I swat Essie on the ass to get her headed toward the bathroom.

As I shut the door behind us, I catch the flash of jealousy and longing etched across Rory's face, and it makes me feel ten feet tall, with an ever-hard, Kline-sized dick.

"One day, you're going to get your ass handed to you." Essie speaks to me via her reflection, while facing the mirror. I'm not sure if she means an angry parent will beat me, or if Rory's going to snap and finally take what I keep offering.

"It'll be worth it," is the answer to both questions. "Let's rinse the chlorine off." Reaching in, I crank the knob to hotter than hell, finding out the honeymoon suite's shower is nothing to write home about.

Shucking my swim trunks, I step into the shower while Essie does her private business. "I need to know that you're okay after what happened earlier today." She's used to me being blunt, so I don't pussy-foot around the issue. "If you're confused, I need to know now."

"Guilty," is Essie's answer. The shower curtain jerking open has me jumping out of my skin. "Sorry," she breathes near my cheek as she steps in behind me. "Didn't mean to spook you."

"Guilty?" I grab for the soap. "I was right there, and so was Beth. If we didn't like it, we would've stopped it. Hell, I'm the one who made you touch each other in the first place."

Nibbling her bottom lip in indecision, Essie borrows the tiny bar of soap from my hand. "Guilty because you didn't play with us, I guess. Ashamed because what would people think."

"Fuck those people," I snarl, voice sharp and lashing. "They aren't living our lives– and if anyone can tell you life is too short, it's me."

Leaning her chest against my back, Essie's arms wrap around my torso. "I get it on an intellectual level, Dev– I do." The soap is spread across my stomach, and my cock rises to the occasion. "I'm confused emotionally, and ashamed morally."

"Ess–"

Essie stops me, grabbing my hands before I can push her away and flip around to look her in the eyes. "Obviously Beth and I have talked polyamory to death, especially after you and Rory got hooked on one another. I get it, Devon. I. Get. It. Just give me time to navigate it, since it's so new to me."

"Are you really okay?" This time Essie allows me to turn to face her. The soap hits the bottom of the tub as my palms cup Essie's face and her hands grip my hips. "Because if you aren't okay with this, we'll stop right now. No more. The last thing I want you to feel is guilt or shame."

"I. Get. It." Essie rises on her tippy toes, pressing her lips to mine, pouring all of her love and understanding deep into my soul. "I love you."

"I love you too," is more of a cry of alarm and joy, than a proclamation of adoration. "I don't want to fuck us up, Ess– not after all I've already put you through. We made vows, and I plan to keep them."

"I made vows too." Holding my gaze, challenging me to witness how serious she's being, "I'd do anything for you. At first, I thought I was being selfless by allowing you to fool around with Rory. Then I realized how badly I needed my best friend, more as a sister and a partner, than someone I called once a day. Then I noticed how well Rory and I fit as we planned the reception."

Rendered speechless, all I can do is marvel at my wife as Essie shows her inner strength. "I. Get. It." She enunciates slowly, making sure I believe her. Then her voice trails off, bashful over what she says next. "I want it too, Dev."

*_*_*

Stepping out of the bathroom, Essie and I share a loaded look, neither one of us sure what we'll encounter on the other side of the door. Donning a pair of pajama pants, and nothing else, I wish I had a hoodie as protection. Essie's wearing a soft nightie, enticing because it leaves more to the imagination– covered or not, her tits and belly can't be disguised.

I'm not going to lie, even though I could and usually do– I'm motherfucking terrified all the sudden. This is going to be a ride of a lifetime, but I'm unsure if the journey is going to take us to Heaven or Hell.

For Essie, for Rory, for Beth, and me, I'm willing to wager our mediocre contentment for the ultimate of happily ever afters.

A small hand fits perfectly into mine as we step out of the bathroom, like two scared children finding more courage facing the unknown together.

A bark of sharp laughter is torn from my throat, as Essie giggles at my side. All that worry, all the freaking out in the bathroom, where Essie and I shared our greatest fears, only to walk out and find Beth and Rory sitting around the coffee table, playing War with a deck of cards.

"You guys squeaky clean?" Beth teases us, because we were hiding out in the bathroom for quite some time, too scared to exit, while also giving Rory and Beth some privacy to talk to each other too.

Essie and I figured that ought to be a rule of ours– privacy within our marriages, within our relationships, within our friendships, within the larger partnership. The right to not have to be an open book, to not be interrogated. The right to our own privacy.

"Feeling brand-spanking new, I'm so clean," I volley back at Beth, unsure what to do or say.

"Who's winning?" Essie's more social than I am, knowing exactly what to say and do. After grabbing the Caffeine-Free Coke we got specifically for her, she makes her way to sit on the sofa next to Rory.

"Nope!" Beth orders from her seat in the rolling desk chair, pointing across the length of the coffee table to where she's pulled an upholstered chair closer. "That's your seat for the night– Dev gets the floor, in between us, opposing Rory."

"Thanks," I mutter dryly, rolling my eyes and thinking of Willow and Ren while I do it. "Always relegated to the floor."

"You're closest to it," Beth taunts me, smirking. "Well, technically Essie is, but it would be rude to make a pregnant woman sit on the floor."

"C. U. N. T." I spell out slowly, like I'm in a spelling bee and it's the word CAT. On my way by the desk, I grab my bottled unsweetened iced tea. Then I feel like a shit, because normally this type of situation calls for alcohol, and Beth is mainlining

Coke, and Rory is double-fisting big bottles of Gatorade. "Thanks. Are we playing War too?"

The slapping of cards continues, until the deck is gone. With Rory and Beth giggling at each other, when they mistakenly try to steal the other's winning hand... on purpose. Cheaters. Essie and I watch, fond smiles locked on our faces.

They must have had a conversation of their own, then rearranged the seating area, as step two in Operation Polyamory is in full swing.

Rory's down to just a pair of soft Jersey cotton boxers, and absolutely nothing else, chest muscles flexing every time he makes a grab for his winning hand. His dick's hard, straining at the front of his shorts, the shape of his meaty head obvious.

Beth's wearing a robe, the curve of her bare tits exposed, with a long line of smooth thigh on display. I never paid much attention when we were in the Playroom, because Beth was always naked and fucking Auggie, and it creeped me out to see my non-blooded uncle's monster dick all the time.

Beth's got a killer body on her, and I'm looking forward to marring it all up with my branding touch.

With a heavy slapping sound on the coffee table, "I win!" Beth hoots in victory, showing how her stack is higher than Rory's.

"Cheater," Rory mutters, humor and affection lacing his voice. "Been a little cheater at all games since I met you."

"Damn straight, Mr. Essex, and don't you forget it." Beth giggles, sorting the cards in the proper direction, so they'll fit back into the box. "We're playing a game, friends," she murmurs slyly, taking over from the plans we made during the flight.

I was to take care of step one, and Beth would do step two, and we'd wing step three, if one and two were a bust.

So far, so good.

While Essie and I share a look of silent communication, Rory ventures over to the bed, while Beth places stacks of folded, hotel-complimentary notepad pieces of paper onto the table. Then a long shadow is cast over me, and I look up to find Rory handing me a pillow.

"Use it as a cushion," Rory whispers softly, the expression on his face one I've never seen before. I could never put a name to the emotion, no matter how hard I might try.

Taking it, unsure of what's going on between us, I lift slightly and pop the pillow underneath my butt. "Thank you," I breathe back just as quietly, eyelashes doing that stupid, fucking fluttering bullshit I can't seem to gain any control over.

That lightning sensation assaults my insides– blood racing, heart warming, face heating, hands sweating. Shaky, but in a good way. It's the sensation of being in love. Not falling in love– it's spiraling out of control down a dark, bottomless pit into the unknown. It's more addictive than the most potent of drugs, perhaps even more terrifying.

The love I have with Essie is as easy as breathing– no doubts, no fears, just a feeling of certainty, comfort, and contentment.

This overpowering, intoxicating sensation Rory drives straight into me, it's like harnessing lightning– the wrongness of it makes it even more gratifying. Wrong, because we're both married to other people. Wrong, because he's my best friend. Yet right because of those same reasons too.

Panting, Rory hitches what breath I do have left by leaning down to press his lips to mine, wordlessly conveying how he's feeling exactly as I am in the moment. Suffocating on uncertainty, yet feeling motherfucking alive because of it.

Still reeling, I sit on the pillow Rory gave me, stupid look on my face, with my eyelashes doing their idiotic dance, as Rory passes out soft, connecting kisses to both the girls, then retakes his seat.

"I know you guys have played this game." Smirking, Beth points the hotel-complimentary pen at Essie and me, and then makes a swirling gesture toward the stacks of paper. "How about you, big boy?"

"Yeah." Rory blushes bright, redder than I've ever seen him do before, and I've seen him in some compromising positions– situations I've placed him in. "In high school."

"While *you* were in high school?" Beth snickers sinisterly. "Or while Rob and Auggie were in high school?"

Catching on, ironic laughter floods out from between my lips. "Good God, do I even want to know the answer to that? I never played this game before, but I've watched enough rounds of it."

I attended a ton of parties in high school, but not because I had any real desire to be there. I'd drink, and that's when I got to know Willow better, during the games that went along with drinking. Drinking was a precursor to fucking, and I didn't fuck.

Drinking wasn't my problem, because I was just waiting for the harder shit to come out after everyone else started fucking, leaving Willow and me to toke up together, along with the rest of the stoners who weren't interested in fucking.

The reason I was at those parties was to keep an eye on Essie, and I watched her give head countless times because of this game, and get fucked once because of it too. I have a loathing relationship with this game.

Essie's looking ashamed, and I'm fuming, and Rory picks up on that quicker than Beth usually does, which is impressive. Beth's not that insensitive, so I assume this is some type of aversion therapy for us.

Lightening the mood again, self-deprecating laughter fills the air, coming directly from Rory. "I partied a lot in high school." Rory practically chokes on his own laughter. "Not mine, mind you... I was working through mine. During Isis, Rob, and Auggie's high school career– I know this game well."

"Did you play it with them?" Essie shudders, skeeved out over the thought of her cousin touching Rory, when Rob's fucked Beth, and he's used his creepy hugging therapy on me, while Essie watched from the shadows.

"Sometimes." Rory blushes brighter. "It was weird though." Now it's Rory's turn to shudder. "Rob instinctively knew to leave me alone, always passing me over. Auggie feared me kicking his ass. Isis and I kissed once, and it was affirmation how there was nothing between us but iron-clad friendship."

"Isis kissed Willow," Essie offers up, shocking all of us, but sickening me more.

Bile rising in my throat. "Eww... my aunt kissed my ex-girlfriend?" Making gagging sounds, "Seriously. Ick."

"Willow also fucked your uncle," Beth mutters matter-of-factly, no judgment. "Before she was with you."

"*I know*," I stress, stomach twisting. "I was there, remember?"

"So was I," Essie meeps out, looking green around the gills herself. "I hid, and then ran away like a coward when I freaked out."

"Oh, my God! Really?" Beth rolls her eyes, using a high-pitched girly voice unlike her own. "Me too! I was there too!"

"I lost my virginity with Auggie watching," I admit, not sure if they knew that.

"Me too!" Rory shouts, mimicking Beth, then begins chuckling darkly. "You sick fucks are disturbing me. Seriously. They're my friends, but they're your relatives. Seriously. Stay the fuck out of the Playroom."

Stretching, arms held high over her head, causing the robe to split open all the way to her belly button, rounded breasts revealed with the nipples still hidden beneath the fabric, Beth's lips curl into a naughty smile. "No relatives of mine…" she drawls out, letting Rory know she'll never stop going to the Playroom.

"We better play the game," Essie and I mutter in unison, after having discussed Beth and the Playroom clientele while hiding out in the bathroom. We decided Beth needed an escort, no matter what, always taking one of us with her when she does her escapades.

"FYI: I've kissed Willow too," Beth announces to get a rise out of us. "Technically, I had sex with her."

Chuckling evilly, I love how mortified Essie looks, and how Rory's dick is about to leap out of his shorts and impale whichever one of us is nearest. "*I know*," I stress, laughter thick in my voice. "I was there, remember? Talk about disturbing to witness… so much for keeping secrets."

With Rory and Essie still mentally out of commission, Beth straightens in her chair, then rolls closer to the coffee table. "Instead of the usual folded papers in a hat version. I've made handy stacks of four– one for each of us." Beth's voice pitches high with glee. "In three rounds. There's no backing out– ya gotta do it."

Since I have the bird's eye view from my position on the floor, I finally notice how the first stack says **Middle School**, the second says **High School**, and the third set says **Adulthood**, all in big, block lettering– Rory's artistic contribution, I presume.

"That's utterly terrifying," I whisper underneath my breath, eyes wide with awe. "This will be interesting."

"We're going clockwise." Beth points her pen at my forehead, clearly in teacher-mode, which was her favorite bossy game we played when we were kids. Teacher and her pupils. Beth also loved to play *Church*, which always ended up with us beating the crap out of each other, because I don't do church. "Since you're sitting at twelve o'clock, you go first, Dev."

"You do realize you gave us assigned seats, right?" Rolling my eyes, I grab for the top piece of paper on the Middle School stack. "Clearly, you stacked the deck."

"Cheater!" Rory and Essie chirp in unison, then fall into a fit of laughter, not getting the gravity of Beth's machinations.

Let's get real, all therapists are born manipulators. I'll call a spade a spade. They talk and lead until you agree with them– that's textbook manipulation and gaslighting, and we can only hope they do it for the greater good.

Beth was born to perform her job, just as I was– both of us masters of manipulation and body language.

Beth just lifts one shoulder in a smug shrug.

Sighing heavily, I unfold the paper, and then bust out laughing as the words form a sentence, and make sense inside my brain. "For more than a minute, kiss the person to your left." Rolling my eyes, I get to my knees, then shuffle over to Beth.

"Totally stacked the deck," I whisper as I come mouth-level with Beth. "I don't know what middle school you went to… because we don't even have a freaking middle school, but they better not be kissing each other in it, 'cuz that would piss off Officer Devon, something fierce."

Holding our gazes, Beth and I smirk at one another, then I move in for the kill. Lips brush, once, twice, and then light on the third time. Beth is surprisingly submissive, allowing me to take the lead.

I thought it would be awkward, kissing Beth. Not too long ago, my world crashed because I kissed Willow, after thinking Essie would be the only person I'd ever kiss in my lifetime. The social construct of only touching the one you love, the one you plan to marry, for the rest of your life, hit me hard. Since Essie, then Willow, I added Rory, and now Beth... as our lips dance, right down to the core of my soul, I know I'll never add anyone else to that short list. I'm not shaming those who are free with their touch– it's just not how I'm built to mentally and emotionally function.

Kissing Beth is difficult, because I'm fighting emotions I refuse to feel– my survival depends on it. Beth and I have always had a love-hate relationship, possessive and jealous over Essie, to the point we'd beat each other silly. As adults, it's hard to hang onto that mindset.

To shift from romantic feelings, I force the kiss to become harder, more urgent, tongues dueling and teeth nipping, because Beth and I can only ever be about fucking when it comes to emotions, and partnership when it comes to life.

Pulling away, my truth is written across Beth's facial expression, reflecting back at me. Uncomfortable with the heavy emotions, I slip my hand along the edge of Beth's robe, sneaking inside to cup her breast.

"You have incredible tits," I mutter in a husky voice, tone beyond genuine. "I never noticed before." Fitting snugly into my palm, the teardrop-shaped tit has a perfect, pebbled nipple. "I'm going to fuck you so rough and hard tonight, you're going to be thinking about it for years to come... if you ever forget, I'm going to fuck you again, harder and rougher... exponentially every time, until you'll never forget the feel of my dick inside you."

There's a rough gasp and a curse, but I ignore the direction they came from as I retake my seat on the pillow Rory kindly offered me. Eyes looking straight ahead, but not at Rory, I place my hands on the coffee table, paper discarded, and wait my turn to enter *High School*.

Clearing her throat, Beth seems speechless, which now has me feeling like a smug asshole. Sucking in large gasps of air, she reaches for her paper. "Feel–" coughing to clear her throat, Beth reaches for my iced tea to wet it.

"Let's try this again, shall we?" Releasing uncomfortable laughter, thighs slightly shifting to rub together, "Feel up the person sitting directly across from you."

Busting a gut, I can barely get out, "And here I thought every one of the pieces would say kiss the person to your left."

"C'mon over, girlfriend." Essie blushes, giggling and biting her lower lip, all the while her tits overflow her own palms. "We just gave each other self-examinations last week, but have at it."

Chuckling underneath her breath, Beth wobbles on unsteady legs around the coffee table, choosing to go behind the sofa to avoid walking past me. "I had to write something interesting, since Dev's was to kiss me, and I kiss Rory every single day… had to be middle school appropriate."

"Don't know what fictitious middle school you're attending, Beth, but it's filled with perverts."

"Not my high school, remember?" Rory volleys back at me, grinning, because he was technically a middle schooler when the wayward ones got ahold of him. "Having K-6th in one building, with 7th-12th across the lot in another, is idiotic, isn't it?"

"That's what I've been saying!" My hands fly up in exasperation. "Why do you think I police the fucking school so hard?"

"Hey!" Beth's sharp voice breaks us out of our bitch-fest. "Got our girl's tatas in my hands, and you're too busy gossiping like Peggy Webster to notice." Rolling her eyes, she squeezes one more time, Essie's tits overflowing her tiny hands, modest nightgown the only barrier. "Lump-free, as always, baby girl– still sore?"

"Pregnancy hormones," Essie grumbles, not even blushing. It was hot for me and Rory, but the girls felt nothing but business as usual. Essie leans forward in her chair, as Beth makes her way back to her seat, "Hey, Dev? Did you somehow forget *I'll just put the tip in* when we were barely fourteen?"

"Busted!" Rory shouts, cackling loudly.

"Burn!" Beth breathes into my face, then falls into her rolling desk chair. "Good Lord, you were a horny little bastard, Dev. Swear to God, Isis was going to go Ramsay Bolton on your Theon Greyjoy ass."

Raising my hands in defeat. "Not gonna lie– that's all true… which is why–"

"You're on the high school like flies on shit," Rory finishes for me. "Naughty boy, you were… still are." Then he leans forward to snatch his paper from the coffee table. "Ha! No big shocker."

Rory doesn't read his task aloud– he just slides off the sofa to his knees, and plants his lips on my wife's mouth. Sneaking a devious look over his shoulder at me, he whispers, "I was a bad boy in middle school too," as a warning. Then his hand is on Essie's tit, stealing another base, lips homing back in.

The wet moans have me rolling my hips to seek relief, and I catch Beth doing something similar out the corner of my eye. Rory gets way into it, mouth working Essie's, one hand on her bare thigh and the other dipping beneath the neckline of the nightie to capture her tit, leaving Essie practically swooning in her chair. A weak whimper escapes my lips, because I know the power of Rory's seduction techniques… and seducing, he is.

Flushed and panting, "Good boy," Beth murmurs with satisfaction and pride, as Rory retakes his seat on the sofa.

The twisted expression of frustration on Rory's face has me chuckling, especially when he plunges his hand down the front of his shorts to adjust his hard-on. He's so fucking hard and meaty and juicy, my goddamn mouth waters.

Directed at Beth, "Is mine the same as yours?" Essie's catching on to the pattern. "Because I just felt your boobs up the other day."

"Nope," Beth shocks us all. "Take your paper."

Leaning forward, Essie snags her task. "Nice…" she drawls out in a rolling purr. "Feel up the person to your right." Curling her finger, Essie calls Rory to her. "Stroked your dick this morning, makes groping your chest seem kinda backward, don't ya think?"

"You and Beth got jipped this round." Rory sways in front of Essie, like a male stripper preparing for a lap dance, hands caressing his own chest. "You wanna touch this, babe? Hmm?" Wiggling his rounded, tight ass for Beth and me, no doubt Essie's getting a view of his dick bobbing around loosely in his shorts. With a hard nipple twist and a grunt, "You can't touch this."

We all laugh in shock as Rory retakes his seat on the sofa, not knowing who that dirty man was, but finding him hot as fuck just the same.

"I wanna know what the front view looked like on that," I murmur to myself. "Hey, look at that–" reaching for the top piece of paper in the High School pile. "Will this be freshman appropriate, or more like the last day of senior year?"

Beth coughs into her hand, not even bothering to hide the snort she was pretending to smother.

"Yeah, now I'm worried," I ramble to myself as I slowly unfold the paper. "Jesus," is a sharp, hissing intake of breath, paper getting rumpled in my clenched fist. "Go down on the person to your left–"

"Well, that escalated quickly," Rory murmurs, amusement and lust warring in his tone.

My eyes snap up, quickly looking from Essie, then to Rory, silently asking for permission.

This first time, doing all these different things, now's the time to put a stop to it if we're uncomfortable, because after this point, permission will be assumed. I will take on no guilt after this, nor listen to a word in a fight where it's used as ammunition against me. If this is going to work, we have to be honest.

"Three seconds, or forever hold your peace," is a warning as I rise up onto my knees. Silently counting in my head, in the breathy silence of our spouses, I knee-walk three steps over to where Beth is sitting in the desk chair.

Palms starting at Beth's ankles, I skate my hands up her shapely calves, between her knees, and then slowly slide along her smooth thighs, parting her legs as far as they will go. Hearing Beth's panting breath, my eyelashes do that fluttering thing, and it disturbs me on many levels.

Not going there… with a rough yank of my hands, fingertips leaving bruising divots, Beth's ass is pulled off the seat. Fingers grappling with the armrests, Beth's trying to keep from spilling to the floor.

Not going to lie, the only girl I've ever gone down on is in this very room, and I did it at first because I wanted my dick sucked. Essie hated sucking my dick, so I would coax her with my tongue. I got good at it in my quest to get head, but I found out I liked giving it better than getting.

I've never even contemplated going down on anyone but Essie. I'd touched Willow, and it was destructive, and painful, and awkward, and barely a brief blip of a night in my existence, one I wish I could erase and never had committed.

I don't want my loyalty to my wife to place Beth in that box labeled *regret*, so I spend a few minutes caressing her legs and whispering kisses along the insides of her thighs, while I have a silent conversation with my emotions and my dick.

My emotions are all over the place, but that's par for the course with me. My dick? Well, it's been forty-eight hours since I got off last. I'm used to waiting to use my one spurt a day until the last minute. Last night, I was saving it for Rory in the bathroom at Rush, during the party, but my dad busted us, and I was too creeped out to use it after that. Since, I've been in a perpetual state of arousal, knowing I needed to use my dick for the big finale of Operation Polyamory.

I don't have the luxury like most men, where I can jerk off to relieve the pressure, then last longer during the main event. If I use it, I'm done, with a refractory rate of nearly twenty-four hours, thanks to the drug regimen that keeps me from harming myself and others.

Not having the unlimited use of my own dick is an annoyance, but not seen as a mark against my manhood. Essie doesn't understand, thinking I don't want her, no matter how many times I try to explain– intellectually, she gets it. Emotionally, Essie's incapable due to her insecurities and sexual hang-ups.

None of that means anything in the grand scheme of things, when my continued existence is at risk. I'm lucky, many of the men taking a similar mix of prescription meds, they can't get an erection at all. We can thank my age, my extreme horniness, and the fact that I'm a Mason for that.

But none of that is my issue right now, as I struggle to get control of myself. Hands massaging the outsides of Beth's legs, offering support, my cheek is rubbing against the creamy skin of her inner thigh, leaving whisker abrasions behind. The scent of chlorine is faint, but not unwelcomed, but it's the musky twang of Beth's arousal that has me seconds away from nutting.

"Hey, Rory!" Beth calls out, but it doesn't startle me. "Why don't you pass me my card, and we'll save it for a few minutes. You take your card and do as it says."

Instinctively, I know exactly what Rory's task is– the same as mine, but with my wife.

"You okay?" Rory's fingertips caress the nape of my neck, concern heavy in his voice.

Beth laughs, jacked up to my emotions, no doubt feeling my panting breath against the inside of her legs. "Dev's just struggling– and not with what you think." A throaty chuckle has my dick pounding, balls pulling tight up against my body. "Somebody didn't get to get off last night, and we've been driving him nuts ever since."

"Quite literally," I murmur wryly, lips fluttering against Beth's skin. "If I pop now, I'll be able to participate, but that's it."

"Oh, shit!" Rory's laughter trills along my spine, then his lips are pressing to the nape of my neck– damp and hot, leaving cooling wetness in their wake. "The bathroom... earlier in bed... Jesus, Dev– I'm so sorry."

"Go eat my wife's pussy," I order in a teasing tone, then add a sharp bite to Beth's thigh to get her to squeal. "Make her come, because your wife's mega-brain will be short-circuiting by the time I'm through with her."

Rory's satisfied chuckle flows away, as he walks over to Essie. I sense it, a second before I hear it, the moment Rory falls to his knees and buries his face between my wife's legs. The guttural sound Essie makes has my hand clenching my junk so hard, I fear I'm going to tear it off and Theon Greyjoy myself.

No jealousy, no possession, because this is Rory touching Essie– Essie touching Rory, while I explore Beth.

It's still a big deal for me, though– more so than sex, I think. In my head, Essie was the only woman for me, and when I touched Willow, it broke something necessary within me. Rory wasn't a complication or a problem, because it was the one-man, one-woman mentality that was fucking me up, and Rory and I were a man and man coming together. It had nothing to do with religion's version of morality, because I'm an atheist. In my head, I wanted what my dad had and lost, and I ruined that reality when I touched Willow. Rory was something on another playing field, something I'm still not sure I understand.

"Not gonna last long if I get too into this," I warn Beth, and no doubt Essie's told her I love to eat pussy. "Hopefully you're keyed up, because I want to get you off. Next time, I'll do this after I nut, and I can go for hours."

"Oh, Jesus." Writhing in the chair, and my lips haven't even touched her yet, Beth proves it won't take much to bring her. But, then again, she's got a view I'm too terrified to glance at, fearing it will make me cream my pants.

I've watched Essie give countless head, seen her get fucked as well as licked, and it was pure torture for the both of us. Essie hated it more than I did, giving her a complex and sexual hang-ups no therapist could fix, ones I could never erase, no matter how much reassurance and sex I give her.

The sounds Rory is pulling out of Essie, my heart softens even more for the man, knowing he's able to do something vitally important for my wife. Those aren't phony porn moans we're hearing. Essie believes Rory wants her, wants to pleasure her, and his thick, meaty cock is the visual proof I can't give her but once a day.

I get it though, how off it would feel to make-out with someone who couldn't physically get turned on. Having someone go down on you, while he's as soft as a grub, unable to get off too, how selfish and guilty that would make a person feel. It turns Essie off, makes her feel unsexy and unwanted and selfish, even though I'm mentally and emotionally aroused, and I want her more than ever. I get Essie, and she gets me, but there is no meeting in the middle on this subject.

Unable to take it any more, with a deep moan, my face presses between Beth's thighs, seeking the musky scent that's driving my balls wild. Just as smooth, hairless, and flawless as Essie, there's no barrier between my lips and the heart of Beth's pussy.

Our moans join the mix, as my lips part Beth's folds, then I get the first taste of another woman on my tongue. Groaning, pressing closer, fist acting as the ultimate of cock rings, I delve deep with my tongue, impaling Beth's pussy— already feeling the rhythmic contractions, the first stirrings of her orgasm.

Beth's fingers twist in my hair, and I sense she's being careful, trying not to key me up too far. The background soundtrack of Rory getting Essie off just about does me in, but it's the taste on my tongue and the thrilling realization I'm eating Beth's pussy, someone who isn't my wife, with my wife and Beth's husband looking on.

It's wrong, in the rightest of rights, and it feeds into my insane need to do very, *very* bad things to feel alive.

Forgoing soft, because I cannot go there with Beth, I bite. I bite hard, lips wrapping around Beth's engorged clit, surprised to see how meaty and large she becomes. Essie's clit is the size of a pea, but Beth's has substance, reminding me of a pinkie fingertip. Sucking, tonguing, my teeth root at the base of the bundle of nerves and bite.

It's the tugging, the pulling slightly away from her body with my teeth, that sets Beth on a collision course. Writhing, rolling chair sliding across the floor, my knees get bruised up as I try to keep up with Beth. Unrelenting, refusing to let me go, Beth's fingernails dig into my scalp, hair breaking off in her fists, as I struggle to keep up with the rolling chair.

Thighs press against the sides of my face, nearly suffocating me, I'm just thankful the chair has stopped moving. Chuckling a sound of pure arrogance, I release Beth's clit and slump back to rest on my knees.

Fluttering my eyes open, panting laboriously, I find out why the chair stopped rolling. Rory's standing behind the chair, hands on his wife's shoulders, a look of pure satisfaction blazing down at me from his gaze.

"And here you said fucking me would be like riding a wild bull," I tease Beth, who's slumped lifeless in the chair, legs parted limply, wet and puffy sex on display. "I forgot all about coming, because that was something else…"

My hand immediately seeks my crotch, hoping to find no dampness. My dick usually takes on a life of its own, because I'm not the nicest to it– downright abusive to it sometimes. Sometimes I don't realize I'm even hard, or that I've spurted, until after the fact. Sighing in relief, I encounter a hard dick and a palmful of precum.

"I–" Swallowing thickly, Beth gestures to the nearest drink. Essie's up from her seat, handing Beth a Coke, because Rory's stabilizing the chair, and I can't move yet. "I… the next two plays are the same thing– not quite what we just did. I planned on doing them one at a time, but that wore me out, so let's do another simultaneous play after I catch my breath… gimme a minute."

"How about…" Rory reaches down to pick Beth up, making it look effortless. I'd be jealous, since I can't pick anyone up without struggling, but I have Rory to do the heavy lifting for me. "You take a time-out on the sofa, and Devon can play with us."

"Excuse me?" Interest piqued, cock bobbing in my pajama pants.

Chuckling, Rory places a lifeless Beth on the sofa, then arranges her arms and legs, propping her up so she can watch us. "If any of us, so much as breathes on your dick, you're done for," Rory states firmly, but wry amusement is tingeing his tone.

"How do you know what the next play is?" Leaning backward, I catch Rory's gaze. "Hmm?"

"Who do you think helped write them out?" Rory flashes me a similar look to the one I'm giving him, and fuck if my dick doesn't almost explode in my pants because of it. I want him under me, over me, *in* me.

Essie and I share a quick look of confusion, unsure of what's happening. We both thought Beth was in charge, and now we discover that isn't the case. I thought it was Beth and me switching off during this weekend, and maybe in life, then Rory has to show his bossy side while Beth's out of commission, and it's confusing the piss out of me.

Balance.

With four of us, one of us will always know what to do in any given situation, picking up the others' slack.

The stress of being in a couple of two, with a kid on the way, meant I was probably going to have to be in charge the majority of the time, with the odds of Essie not knowing what to do when I didn't was quite high. With two people, there was too much room for error, where neither one of us knew what was up from down. I'm not a know-it-all. I'm strong-willed and intelligent, but I fuck up– *often* –and I'm not sure I could survive the guilt of those fuck-ups.

"It's your turn in the chair," Rory mutters wryly, helping Essie sit in the rolling desk chair. Eyebrow hitching high in challenge, he looks down at me. "Maybe I wasn't asleep on the flight… maybe you were whispering, but I'm so attuned to the sounds of your voices, I picked up on the gist of it all… *maybe*." Lips curling, Rory reaches down to pull me to my feet. "Maybe I've just been going along with your plan, because I already knew what you had planned."

"Shit," I hiss with feeling, face glowing beet-red in a nanosecond. The blood loss, as it all channels to my face and junk, has my knees wobbly weak.

Rory snags the last piece of paper in the *High School* pile, and hands it to Essie. "For you, me lady," he says with a flourish. "Don't read it aloud– we're gonna fuck with Devon's head for a minute."

"Hey!" I grumble in protest. "My head's already fucked– there ain't no fucking it up more than it already is."

To the background soundtrack of Essie's sadistic giggling– whatever's on that paper is something else –Rory leans down to whisper into my ear, heavy palm clasping the nape of my neck. "I'm so goddamn horny, all I want to do is come right now– this task won't last long, or I won't last to Adulthood."

"Yeah, I'm feeling ya on that." Hand cupping my crotch, fingers tightening. "It's like sexual gymnastics for pros, but I need to be in the beginner's class, where we just jerk off together and come in less than three minutes."

"I don't have three minutes in me," Rory warns, pointing at the large damp spot spreading on the front of his shorts, dick loosely bobbing beneath the fabric. "Because I know what's coming next."

"Shit," I hiss, eyes going wide. "That's why Beth's resting up?"

"No shit, Officer Devon– it's about to get real."

Eyes nearly popping out of my skull, I watch as Essie unbuttons the top of her nightie, then parts the sides to allow her tits to flow out. So large, she has to lift her breasts out of the top of her nightgown, fully exposing herself. A flush pinking her skin, with stiff nipples, Essie is aroused and ready for more.

"Come stand behind my chair, Dev." Essie bats her eyelashes at me, all the while holding her own tits in the palms of her hands. "Pretty please," she begs, and my cock is no longer threatening to ejaculate… it's going to happen, whether I stimulate it or not… like it or not. "Stabilize the chair, and hold these suckers together for me."

It takes the short walk around the chair for my mind to finally register what Essie said. "Holy shit! Whose deviant mind thought this one up– Christ, I wish I thought of it." Leaning the back of the chair against my chest and the front of my hips, I reach around to cradle Essie's tits together. Their heavy weight is as comforting as it is erotic for me.

Rory points at his bare chest, lips curled into the smuggest of smirks. "Me." Then he drops trou. As I wig out, happy to use the chair for support, so I don't land on my ass, Rory keeps talking as if seeing him buck-ass naked isn't doing wicked things to me.

"All me. We were supposed to use both of our wives, but tonight has been too stimulating." Rory walks toward us, cock flopping from hip to hip like a lust-fueled metronome. Us, and it is *us*– Essie *and* me. "We'll do that next time."

"Next time?" I gulp out, unsure if I can survive our future sexcapades.

Rory just smirks up at me, knowing better than to touch me right now, because my dick couldn't take it. With utter concentration, and a wicked light shining from his gaze, Rory rubs the head of his dick between Essie's breasts, each pass delving deeper and deeper into the crevice she's created.

"Open your mouth, baby," I coax in a crooning voice down at Essie, and she looks up at me with utter trust from her zealot gaze. "When Rory's cockhead gets close, lick it… see if you can suck it."

"Oh, my God!" Rory stops working his cock, as rolling waves shudder along his spine. "You two aren't playing fair."

"Don't let the devious one join in the shenanigans if you want it to be vanilla," I warn, chuckling over how traditional Rory can be sometimes. Deep down, Rory's naughty, downright filthy, but he's scared of the Playroom and everything it represents.

"Last week, when we were discussing which of my DJs to use for the party…" voice sluggish, almost sounding drugged, Rory continues to press his dick between Essie's tits, leaving a wet trail of precum to glisten in the light. "This–" Rory slips in between her tits, then does a practice thrust upward. "The thought of doing this to you, while Devon watched… it popped into my head so violently, I had to get up and go jerk off before we could continue our planning."

Whimpering, my hips lean heavily on the chair, moving us several inches, as my fingers tighten on Essie's flesh, pressing Rory's dick between the soft globes. Essie does just as I bid, tongue sneaking out to snatch a bead of precum as Rory's dick nears her chin.

"I was so fucking hot when Rory told me about it." Beth's regaining her strength, eyes lasered in on the action. "I rode Rory's cock while he told me about wanting to titty-fuck Essie while you helped, Dev."

"Jesus fucking Christ." Dropping Essie's tits like we're playing a perverted version of Hot Potato, I take a giant leap backward, hand delving deep into my pants as I move. Twisting, I brutalize my dick to stop it from erupting.

"I don't know if I'm gonna survive us," I warn, and I don't just mean tonight.

"I promised to keep your life interesting." Flushed, sweat beaded on his forehead, Rory's struggling almost as badly as I am. "Read the only task in the *Adulthood* pile, Dev."

Leery, I reach for the last piece of paper on the coffee table. "Just so we're clear… whatever this says, don't expect my performance to be stellar. You know I come to a point where I can't edge off the orgasm any longer, and my dick gains a mind of its own."

"Same problem, Dev– I've got the same problem going on." Rory rests one hand on my shoulder, fingers clenching and releasing in a comforting, massaging rhythm, while he flicks the paper I'm holding in my hand with the other. "We can back off if you're not sure, or not ready, or never want to go there. This isn't Pandora's box, Dev– it can be opened, closed, reopened, and relocked."

"I want to go there," I whisper the truth as I unfold the piece of paper to reveal the last barrier of us being in a polyamorous relationship. "Just too keyed up to make it good."

Lips pressed to my ear, Rory whispers for only me to hear. "Beth's more keyed up than you are." Then he steps away, leaving me with the only piece of paper that has his handwriting on the inside.

Fuck my wife while I make love to yours.

Breath shuddering out in a gust, the relief makes my knees weak. It's not that Rory can't fuck Beth– he can, and he does. He's just too soft to do it hard enough for her– make it thrilling, and maybe a touch scary. It's not that I can't make love to my wife– I can, and I do. It's that sometimes I need to be rough, and Essie's not built that way... and that need feeds into her insecurities over me not having a hard-on while we touch.

I zone out a bit, while Rory and Essie get comfortable on the bed. While I pick up the pieces of paper– planning on saving them, because I'm a sentimental shit sometimes –Beth watches me from the sofa.

Stalling, but not because I don't want to go forward with this, I figure I'd give Rory a head-start on me, so we could finish up around the same time. Because, I'm not fucking around, one touch, and I'm going off like a goddamn missile from a rocket launcher.

With no more busy work, I gaze down at Beth as she looks up at me– just two frenemies from the playground, all grown up now and getting ready to fuck for the first time, while our spouses make-out on the bed, holding a soft, murmured conversation in between kisses and caresses.

Without a word, I reach down for Beth's wrist and yank her off the sofa, getting a sick thrill when she squeals in shock. Stronger than I look, manhandling Beth with jerking movements toward the foot of the bed, I shove her as hard as I can to the mattress. Anticipating how I need her to be, Beth is ass-up and face-down on the bed, waiting for anything I'm willing to deliver.

With a harsh yank, I rent the robe right off Beth's back, her body bowing with the force of the movement. The guttural groan she releases spurs me forward, to harder, harsher places.

Channeling all my sexual frustrations, all my inadequacies, all the pain Beth and I have caused each other during our physical and cerebral battles, all that jealousy and possessiveness, my hand flies back to swat her ass so hard, my palm will still be stinging into next week.

The ear-splitting scream has the couple at the head of the bed freezing, eyes going wide in terror. Arching a wry brow in their direction, I don't look away from Beth's pussy, as it's displayed before me like an offering. My fingers delve deep, scooping up fingertips' worth of arousal pumping out of Beth's cunt.

"Don't worry about us," I warn, showing off my glistening fingertips, cream dripping down to my wrist. "Just giving Beth what she's been looking forward–" Beth's needy moan interrupts yet confirms what I am saying.

A never-ending landscape of pale flesh just waiting for my marks. Possessed– or, perhaps, I'm finally feeling self-possessed –my hand flies out time and time again, landing on Beth's jiggly ass and the backs of her thighs, leaving red brands behind. I don't stop until my hand can't take it anymore.

Beth's writhing, sobbing on the edge where pleasure meets pain, body trying to get what I'm not willing to give yet. "No, ya don't," I warn, jacking Beth up onto her knees. "No rutting off on the sheets– you always cheat when we play games."

Rory's muted chuckles have me relaxing some, because I feared showing him this side of me– this side of Beth. When it comes to sexual gratification, Rory truly is vanilla, thinking what we do together is naughty because we're both men, when that couldn't be farther from the norm. Us playing at polyamory right now, even that's vanilla, when Essie and Rory see it as edgy. Essie's of a similar mindset to Rory, proving none of us are truly compatible within our marriages.

In the Playroom, I was always enthralled, and half pissed at myself for wanting it so much. I'd be hard as a rock, but getting off wasn't even a factor for me. It was about power. Back then, I didn't remember all the details of the nightmare, but my therapists have worked with me until I understood why what drew my attention captivated me in the first place.

"Your skin looks goddamn gorgeous right now." Fluttering my lips across the welts my hand left behind, I dampen the emotions I'm feeling.

I can't go there with Beth. I am possessive. I am jealous. If I allowed my emotions to run rampant, I would cut her goddamn hands off if she touched anyone not on this bed. If Beth plans on being active in the Playroom, we can't go anywhere but where we're going now.

Focusing on Rory and Essie on the bed, I watch as they kiss, their breathy moans doing insane things to me, forcing me to feel for Beth what I'm trying so hard to deny.

Hand biting into Beth's upper arm, I hold her upright, all her weight centered on her knees, as I stand behind her on the floor. "How does that make you feel?" I breathe into Beth's ear, directing her gaze to Rory and Essie on the cusp of making love.

Rory senses our attention, eyes flicking up to meet mine first, then Beth's, in a questioning look. He receives the answer he's seeking. Rolling Essie onto her side, Rory spoons her from behind, making sure she's comfortable. With Beth and me looking on, Rory enters my wife, and the sound they create together just about brings me to my knees. Rory's eyes close in pleasure. Essie's back arches in bliss.

"Fuck!" Beth whispers, body losing its ability to hold her upright. If not for my hand on her arm, she would have fallen face-first into the mattress.

"Yeah, that's what we need to be doing right now," I mutter wryly in Beth's ear, then gift her with a punishing nip to the lobe. "Fucking."

Jerking my pajama bottoms off, I step out of them, flinging the fabric off my heel. Then I press my naked body along the back of Beth's, aligning us perfectly. Cock wedging between her butt cheeks, I slide slickly down to her cunt.

"Shit!" Eyes rolling back into my skull, there's no way in hell I'm going to make it inside Beth before I shoot at this rate, especially with the sounds of ecstasy filling the air. "Condom," I hiss, releasing Beth to stride over to our bags.

Laughing, Beth falls to the bed, landing on her cheek, unable to support herself. Ass high in the air, Beth's pussy is pumping out cream– thighs glistening invitingly. The sight *kills* me, dick hammering against my stomach with every heartbeat.

With a shaking hand, I roll the condom on, too keyed up to be patient. The condom is necessary for many reasons. The first being how I'm a Mason– birth control may not be enough. The next being, how if I come inside Beth, my emotions might follow, and that would be to our destruction. Lastly, maybe I'll last a few strokes, numbed slightly by the latex sheathe.

"Let's try this again," I warn in a harsh voice, in juxtaposition to the hand softly caressing the curve of Beth's spine in an upward trajectory. Fingers slide through her thick strands, being gentle to confuse Beth to my true purpose.

With a harsh yank, I jerk Beth upright by the hair, with all the force my strength allows. Beth fights me, slumping to the bed, trying to get me to pull her hair harder. Panting breathlessly, cunt drenched, Beth rears her ass upward, seeking the cock poking her hip.

"Please," Beth begs, tone needy, body language even louder than her voice. "Fuck me... *please.*"

Rory and Essie reached their fevered pitch while I was struggling to get the condom on. Now they're drowsy, gazing at us with slitted eyelids, no doubt curious to see how this will play out.

Knowing I won't last long, I realign myself to the back of Beth's body, using her hair to drag her up to her knees. With my feet planted firmly on the floor, I pull Beth until she's kneeling at the edge of the bed, her back to my front.

Whispering fiercely, the words barely audible, because they are only meant for Beth to hear. "Look at them." Shifting my hips, I wedge my cock between Beth's wet slit, notching myself so my head will rub along her engorged clit.

"Someday, you're going to come to me in bed, and you're going to beg me for something more than a rough fuck," I warn, but it's definitely a promise. I feel it with sincerity down to my bones. "Someday, Rory and Essie are going to give us a blue-eyed baby boy, and we're going to name him Devon."

"Christ!" Beth hisses, alerting Rory to the fact that I'm saying something important, not just filthy, dirty talk.

"Bethany..." I sing sinisterly into her ear, my Masonhood never more powerful. I release Beth's hair, catching her by the tit before she falls face-first to the mattress. Leaving fingertip bruises in the fragile flesh, I skate down to cup her tummy.

"You're going to grow a baby in this belly... *someday,*" I threaten, voice harsh, cock nudging at her entrance. "His name will be Rory." With a rough thrust, I enter Beth as hard as I possibly can.

Beth's gasping silence rings louder than if she had screamed.

Frozen still, the only thing that moves on me is my lips against Beth's earlobe. "Rory Junior will be *my* son," I promise, causing Bethany to fracture apart beneath me...

...and then I fuck her, pouring all my sexual frustration, and that possession and jealousy into it– it's punishing and angry, and I last far longer than I expected. Long enough to turn Rory on to the point he takes Essie again... and I still last, bringing Beth again and again, until she's sobbing for me to come. When I finally finish, it's as if I've never come before in my entire life.

CHAPTER SIX

Half asleep, face pressed against a hard chest, the activity around me doesn't pull me fully awake. My life schedule is firm— between missing a full night's sleep, and the emotional toll of forging this new partnership, it's going to take a crane to yank me out of this bed before I'm physically ready.

"What are your plans?" the chest beneath my cheek rumbles, a heavy palm landing to cradle the back of my head. "Do you want me to text you when we venture out?"

"Yeah, that'll work." Beth's voice sounds distant, with the zip of a bag in the background. "We're going to grab a quick bite and a coffee for breakfast, then hit the stores. Maybe we'll meet up for a meal between lunch and dinner?"

"Hey, Ess!" Rory calls out, modulating his voice, like he's trying not to wake me. "Buy something, okay?"

"You calling me cheap?" I mutter wryly, mouth curling into a smirk against Rory's bare chest, wiry hair tickling my lips. I have no idea how I got into this position, since I fell asleep, last night, spooning my wife, but I'm not complaining. "Or, are you calling me controlling?"

"Both," comes from three different directions, and the chest beneath my cheek rises and falls rapidly with laughter. "This is our first trip together— the girls need to commemorate it with some shopping."

Hand reaching out blindly for my wife, Essie meets me half way. With our fingers tangled, I pull her down to me, eyes barely cracked open. "Buy whatever you want— I trust you not to go overboard."

"Nice warning, ya controlling cheapskate," Rory teases me as I flutter a kiss to my wife's laughing lips.

"Love you— have fun," I murmur drowsily, eyes slamming back shut.

Essie's, "You too," has my eyes popping wide open, then closing when I assume she means she loves me too.

I drift in and out every few minutes as Rory asks and answers questions from the girls. Sounds from the bathroom diminish, to the point I don't hear the door to the hallway open and close as they leave. Sighing, Rory snuggles me closer, then his breathing deepens and evens out.

Body asleep, mind spinning– that's my normal– I mull over the events of the past few weeks, from reconnecting with Rory, up until last night. Other than a night of watching movies and fooling around, we've kept things separate and private.

If last night is the gauge for how our future will play out, will it be heterosexual shenanigans between the four of us, with Rory and I keeping our distance? Is that what the girls need and want, because they don't want to touch each other? I don't want to feel as if we're swingers swapping wives– I thought this would be the four of us.

Together.

Rory and I didn't touch when we watched movies– the girls intercepted me, not letting me suck Rory off. Was that with a purpose? –and we didn't touch last night. In the weeks between, we've only *hugged*, coming the closest to something more in the bathroom at Rush, before Dad interrupted us.

I want this– I want us all together, but not at the expense of losing that connection to Rory.

"You're thinking too loud," the chest is speaking to me again. Heavy palm moving, fingertips start rubbing my scalp. "If I talk enough, maybe you'll wake all the way up this time."

"Are you bored?" When did I become an insecure shit? "You can chase the girls down and spend some money with them." Rory has more zeros in his bank account, and he spends his money more easily than I do, without fretting and feeling guilty.

Beth and I are money-misers, with Essie the irresponsible one, and Rory the one with an unlimited cash flow, since Rush has paid his housing costs for nearly a decade.

Large hands reach down to hook my armpits, then I'm being pulled from my nest. I find myself draped across Rory's chest, forehead to forehead. "I'm not bored, dumbass." The words are taunting, but the tone is filled with pure affection.

Rory gazes at me, smiling as my eyelashes do their dance. "I was quite content, waiting for you to wake up."

"Oh, did you want to talk?" I practically gulp out the words, swallowing continuously. Nervous? Why the hell is Rory making me so nervous all the sudden?

Is this the insanity teenagers feel when they have a crush? Because Rory makes me batshit crazy.

Those hands hook on the back of my thighs, shifting me to straddle Rory's hips, and I discover we're both buck-ass naked. A firm chest cushions mine, the wiry hairs scratching at my nipples.

The only difference between us, Rory's cock is thick and juicy, whereas mine is a tiny, hibernating grub, no matter how badly aroused I am inside my own head.

There's another difference, though… Rory understands how my cock's inability to become engorged is not indicative of my hunger for him.

Palms rest on the back of my skull, fingers splayed until my entire head is enveloped. Rory pulls me down to his lips, kissing me the way we did in the bathroom. A crazed mashing of lips, bodies igniting, as we grope whatever we can reach.

Hungry whimpers flow out my mouth to spill into Rory's, begging for things I can't put into words. Somehow understanding, Rory doesn't take his time with me, not after last night. It was so drawn out, I thought I'd explode before we got to the good stuff. But, last night was about getting to know us as a polyamorous partnership. It wasn't about the individual relationships within the greater partnership.

This is Rory and me, and we're impatient men, needing instant gratification. There's something we can do together, instead of me just jerking or sucking him off, that doesn't require me to have an erection, and we both want it.

"I can't wait any longer," Rory practically sobs out in warning, reaching for a bottle of lube he had stashed beneath the pillow underneath his head. "I can't– I'm going fucking nuts."

"Kiss me," is a pleading moan, as my lips seek out his. "Do whatever the hell you want to me, Rory– I want it too."

"I..." Hesitating, Rory pulls me back, so he can look me in the eyes. "I'm scared– I don't want to hurt you, and I don't want what happened to you to flare back up and taint this for us."

"I don't think–" Everything I've discussed with many therapists in the past few months rushes back in on a comforting wave. Rory's not saying no, he just wants to know the boundaries.

"I might never be able to take it from behind– never kneeling on the floor, never with my chest pressed to a chair... Alejandro didn't harm me. Even though I know it was rape, I still felt as if I had a say. A choice. A semblance of power. He made it feel good, Rory. That's the mindfuck. He made me come... I know I'll love this with you– I'm not scared it will hurt. I'm not worried I'll freak out," it spills out of me in a rush, followed by a begging plea, "Just touch me."

Taking me at my word, Rory kisses me again. This time it's more fervent, bodies on fire. Mewing, and I'm not ashamed to admit that, I rub every inch of my flesh against his, rocking my hips up in the air, begging him to touch me.

Those large palms grab my ass, tugging and releasing, causing me to rock against the hard length jutting against my pelvis.

My brain says I'm hard, even though I know I can't be. That's another mindfuck I have to live with, my brain and body miscommunicating. I'm so turned on, it's impossible for my brain to reconcile with the fact that I'm not as hard as a motherfucking steel rod. My actions and reactions are those of someone who is in the throes of ecstasy, not that of a guy with a soft cock.

Gasping for breath, tongue dragging from the depths of Rory's mouth, I rest my face against his throat... and I just experience it all. Experience the rough way Rory is handling me, a way he'd never touch the girls. I'm not fragile– he knows I can take it. How raspy his breathing is against the side of my face. The way his cock jerks and spasms as I wiggle my pelvis against it. The way his calloused fingertips tug my ass cheeks apart, preparing to give me the touch I've been begging to receive.

"Can't wait," is a threat as those questing hands vanish. "Sorry." The lube is squeezed, drenching my crack in sticky wetness. The cold, sluggish trickle has my muscles turning taut. "If I hurt you, we'll go back to my fingers… or I can rim you. But I… but I can't wait any longer, Dev– I feel fucking nuts."

Draped over Rory's body, I'm a heck of a lot smaller than he is, and that's the only reason this position works. From on top, I'm in a position of power and control, even though he's doing all the work, because I'm spaced out on lust.

A finger penetrates me, tearing a sharp grunt from my chest, while the other hand is busy grabbing the base of Rory's cock. "Just breathe out with me," Rory requests, finger disappearing with his cockhead replacing it. "Ready?"

Before I can reply, all the breath in my lungs expels in a large gust, as Rory pushes his way home. Hands hold my hips, waiting for me to adjust. Rory's better at this than he realizes, his ability to read body language.

As soon as my eyes unroll from the back of my skull, Rory begins moving me up and down, using his hands on my hips to guide us. We go slow, letting me get used to the invaded sensation, the burning sting that has every nerve in my body zinging and my skin tightening.

Panting, I sit up, needing to see Rory's facial expressions as we fuck for the very first time. Palms resting on his pecs as leverage, I take over, turning Rory into my passenger.

"Good?" is barely audible from my lips, as I gaze down at the stupefied expression on Rory's face. He's finally developed that eyelash flutter, cheeks flushed with arousal, lips swollen and crimson from our kisses.

Body quivering beneath mine, dick jerking inside me, "Arghung…" is a nonsensical word, which I take to mean Rory's doing goddamn good beneath me.

The discomfort is still there, but I find myself needing to go faster, to chase that sparking sensation as Rory's dick hits me in just the right spot. Faster, faster still, my fingertips dig into Rory's chest as I plunge myself up and down his dick, at a dizzying rate.

Mouth open in a continual moan, eyelids sagging with pleasure, the stuttering stops and starts kick in, where it's impossible to move in a smooth rhythm. I'm moving so fast, my balls pound against Rory– the flash of pain adding to the experience.

"Not gonna…" is all Rory can get out, fingertips tightening on my hips, helping me slam as hard as humanly possible down on his dick. "…laaaaaaaaaast…" is drawn out, followed by a series of grunts in conjunction with bucking movements.

Slumping forward, Rory taking all my weight, we turn into a mass of twitching body parts that can be heard several rooms away, and probably all the way down the hallway too.

"I seriously just came from every cell in my body… Each orgasm I have is stronger than the last…" panting against the side of Rory's throat, I chuckle as his softening dick pops out my asshole, a flood of hot dampness following. "I don't think I can survive the next round."

"Nap," is all Rory is capable of saying, arms clasping me to his chest, not letting me go, even if I tried to fight him.

I wait him out, mind mulling over how everything is more intense with Rory. My emotions are raw with him, as if they're new emotions I'm not used to feeling.

Maybe I'm not the person I used to be. The person who fell in love with Essie and befriended Beth. I know I'm not the person I was, the one who lived in a drugged haze, between the normal, pre-nightmare me, and the wounded one who is finally recovering from the nightmare.

That didn't change who I am intrinsically, but maybe it did change what I want and need to survive. Maybe this insanity I'm feeling with Rory is so intense because it's new and raw, both because it's happening right now, and because my emotions are new and raw to me.

"You're thinking too loud again," Rory warns, arms clenching me tighter. "Talk to me."

"Are the girls going to pretend, like there is no me and you?" I blurt out what has been bugging me. "Because there is a difference between polyamory and wife-swapping."

"So you're the expert, now? You just learned that word yesterday." Chuckling deviously into my ear, Rory squeezes me tighter and tighter, knowing how comforted it makes me.

Safe.

"Dumbass," he purrs with affection. "They left on purpose, to give us privacy, because this *is* private between us."

"Oh," I mumble, feeling like an ungrateful asshole.

"Maybe someday we'll be comfortable doing more than fooling around when we're with them, but it's going to be a long while." Rory kisses my temple, lips lingering. "I like having you all to myself, but it's been hard with you sharing a house with Willow and Ren, and my place being at Rush. I don't want to sneak around, but I do want privacy."

"Good," spills out in a rush, thrilled and relieved to have my fears squashed. "I want that too."

"What else do you want?" Rory shifts beneath me, thick thigh dislodging me, until both of my legs are cradled between his. "It's a negotiation."

"I want to go to a lawyer," comes out of nowhere, mind supplying the information from my subconscious, when I didn't realize it was something I wanted.

"The way I grew up– the way my dad and Isis did, I don't want that for our kids. If it wasn't for the blue wall protecting Dad after my grandpa died– thank God it was a different era back then. Dad was only seventeen, and could have lost the house and Isis, but people stepped up and protected him, vouched for him. That's why Dad married my mom, because it emancipated him, allowing him to make adult decisions."

"That's why?" Rory voice pitches high with shock. "Malcolm was a dang baby– Jesus!"

"Dad was a seventeen-year-old kid, and Isis was only seven or eight at the time, I believe. Dad's only thought was how to keep Isis. I know there's a lot to the story, and Dad, Isis, and Auggie zip their lips tighter than your asshole."

"Ha-ha," Rory mock laughs, swatting me on the ass. "Very funny. Next time we'll see how tight it is… God, no wonder you need the comfort and security of structure," Rory muses, fingertips fluttering down my back lightly, swirling on their way.

"My grandfathers were like Dad and Colin– chief and his second-in-command, with Seth Webster their third. Grandpa Berry had two daughters, and Peggy was determined they would marry her son– Willow and the twins' dad, Sam –and my dad. Dad, Sam, and Ginny were best friends, with my mom slightly older than them. Peggy had it all worked out. Sam and Ginny, and my dad and mom."

"You knew Willow's dad?" Rory sounds shocked, arm clenching around me.

"Probably as well as Willow did, actually," I mutter, remembering how Dad was more upset by Sam's death than Mom's. "No way was Ginny marrying Dad, too much like incest with them being best friends. So Grandpa Berry practically gave my mom to my dad, honoring his partner's son, just so Dad could keep the house and Isis. Then with mom's illness and Dad being in Boston, we were shuffled between my grandparents and Dad– Isis too, and she wasn't even related to them. Then they passed away too… then Mom offed herself… and it fucked Isis up just as much as it did us kids."

"You don't have to worry about that," Rory tries to reassure me. "None of us are like that. Our situation is completely different."

"I need structure, Rory– it's the cornerstone of my recovery. There can't be any gray areas. We need to go to a lawyer. It's not about in the event something happens to me or Essie– I want it about everyday life. You and Beth should be able to walk into Will's school, or take him to the doctor. If something happens to us, I don't want you to have to fight my dad or my billion siblings for your right to be his dad."

"Jesus," Rory hisses, the hitching in his breath a good indication I just emotionally kneed him in the junk. "You want me to be Will's dad?" The arms somehow manage to squeeze me tighter. "Okay. *Thank you.*"

"There's no halfway, Rory– we're either all the way in, or we're not doing it at all. It's not just our emotions, but our future children. I don't give two shits about the townsfolk, or even our relatives. But the kids will have a stable environment, no revolving door."

"I'm all in," Rory vows, voice solemn. "Beth's probably the right person to research this for us. We'll give her a list of demands, and she'll take care of it."

"Okay. Good." A funny, little laugh trickles out my throat, pure relief. "What about you? Anything you want to negotiate?"

"Well…" Rory trails off, voice light and teasing. A smile flirts with his lips, like he has a secret and can't wait to share it. "A mystery was solved while we were having sex, but I don't know if I should tell you."

Eyes narrowed, I growl directly into Rory's face.

Hands push at my chest, and I fear I've gone too far with the threatening behavior. But Rory's laughter has me relaxing, moving where Rory pushes me. Resting on my knees, I have no idea why he unglued us.

"What?" confusion rings in my voice. "Was I squishing you, or something?"

"Look at my stomach." Rory smiles like he just wagered his life-savings, and managed to win the jackpot. "What do you see?"

"Cum." I answer without hesitation, noticing the sticky shit all over my chest and stomach, and glued into the intriguing ridges of Rory's abs and matted into his pubes. "So?"

"Where's my cum, Dev?" he challenges me, arching a brow.

Getting surly from a lack of food and the need of a thorough scrubbing, "Currently dripping out my ass, why?"

"Why is there cum on your stomach?" Rory swipes a finger across my stomach, dipping into my belly button. He laughs in my face, thinking my confusion hilarious. "I'd wondered, ya know? Even discussed it with Beth. Is your long refractory period because of your meds? Because of a mental block? A combination of both?"

"You think my doctors haven't gone over this with me?" I snarl, lashing out because I'm embarrassed and feeling inadequate.

"You were *way* into riding my cock," Rory murmurs, beyond amused, maybe a bit cocky thrown in there for good measure. "I was watching as you Pogo Stick-ed my dick, your cock bouncing off your stomach, practically hammering your belly button, and you didn't even notice."

"Yeah, so?" I'm still not catching on, and it's pissing me the fuck off.

"You looked unbelievably hot, by the way… I think I found a solution." Yep, Rory's definitely feeling cocky and smug. "It might not work every time, but nailing your gland seems to spark your dick back to life."

"What?" I glare down at the offending grub nestled in a thatch of cum-speckled hair. "I loved your dick in my ass– not gonna lie on that point."

"Not my cum, Devon." Rory grabs me, yanking me back down to lie on top of him. "Not my cum… *it's yours*."

CHAPTER SEVEN

"I'm so glad it's me and you." Bumping into Rory on purpose, I walk kind of zig-zagging, trying to get closer to him. "I loathe shopping with a passion." We part to allow a bus group of elderly gamblers to pass.

Coming shoulder to shoulder with me, almost like we're magnetized. "I kinda like shopping," Rory says sheepishly, probably feeling like I'm judging him.

"We can go back." I point behind us, to the store Essie and Beth have been in for the past hour. "You can poke around, and I'll just lurk."

"I'm good." Rory bumps into me on purpose, trying to touch me. "I don't mind fifteen minutes of shopping if it's a store with stuff I like, but the girls are neck-deep in the dressing room right now, and that is boring as fuck."

"Unless it's a lingerie store." Elbowing Rory in the ribs, a fantasy weaves into my head. We part again, this time for a group of rowdy bachelor partiers. "Wouldn't mind you trying something on for me," I whisper out the side of my mouth, voice dripping with lust.

In reply, Rory just makes a growling sound low in his throat, while eyeing me from head to toe. "Yeah... *that*," he whispers back. "Let's walk until we find a store that sells that kinda stuff."

"Game," I mutter, eyes flicking everywhere, looking for a place that sells men's undergarments. "I think you're still hot from that Porsche."

"The guy let us touch it!" Excited, Rory flips around to walk backward, so he can face me while gesturing animatedly. "I'd go back and beg for a test-drive, but he'd probably think I was a stalker."

"I popped mental chub while in Gold & Silver Pawn Shop." Grinning, a shudder works its way down my spine. "I took a gloating selfie and sent it to Willow– she's addicted to Pawn Stars."

"Whole time we were in there, all I thought about was Auggie, but I wasn't sure if I could call him." Face shuttering the emotions he's feeling, Rory looks blankly at me.

"I get it." I quickly reach out to hook my pinkie with his, then immediately drop it. "Auggie's been haunting the back of my mind– I promised not to call Dad, but I texted him earlier, just needed to know everything was okay. Auggie's fine."

"Did you see Auggie's stepdad?" Rory pauses, tugging me close to a store front, so others can pass while we chat.

Rory and Essie are each other's spirit animals.

Gossips.

"It's the first time I've ever seen him– did you get a real, good look at him?"

"I… I-I…" stuttering, I'm not sure how I'm going to get out of this trap, so I'm bluntly honest instead. "In a way, I've been in the Kline family my whole life, Rory. So this is hard, because I want to talk to you, but I don't want to break Tina's confidence. All I can say is that you're going to have to talk to Auggie."

"You know?" Rory's vivid eyes pop wide in awe, and his reaction has me relaxing. I'm relieved Rory will respect me and not get bent out of shape if I deny him, but even more relieved he already knows their dark secret, so I have someone I can talk to about it. "I guessed, between Beth's anonymous case study and when I finally set sight on Patrick."

"Dad and Lisa had this bizarre custody agreement over Auggie, because every time Auggie went home, he'd run away back to our house. Patrick used to drag Auggie out of my house, fuming mad, because Auggie could be a real puke to Lisa… so I know what the guy looked like before he turned white-haired."

Chuckling, I've heard stories about Dad beating the piss out of Auggie. In turn, Auggie would beat the ever-loving hell out of me, but not as badly as he'd go after Ren.

Smirking fondly, "I'm guessing it was Auggie who turned Patrick's hair white in the first place."

"Yeah, but…" Now Rory looks confused. "It was the hair that got me–"

"Patrick's hair used to look like his mom's, now it looks like everyone in his dad's family."

"I'm right!" Rory's mind is blown. "Jesus Christ."

"I snapped a bunch of pictures for Auggie back at the Pawn Stars place," I change the uncomfortable subject. "I'll send them to him in a few days. Patrick would have loved it in there too. Patrick was way into D&D back in the day, and that's how Auggie and Toby got hooked, especially on fantasy video games. Revamped. I think that's why Auggie fell for Willow when he shouldn't have."

"Willow tripped all of Auggie's geeky triggers." Rory grins at me, eyes flicking to the sign above my head. "I think we stopped here for a reason, Dev– do you trust me?"

"Always," I mutter breathlessly, not a moment's hesitation. A split-second later, Rory's tugging me inside the store. "Oh, fuck... I hope I didn't speak too soon. Tattoos?"

"We've talked about it." Rory eyes me, patient and kind, waiting for me to make the decision for the both of us. We're both virgins. "Auggie's tattoos are great. Ya know his back piece?"

"Yeah?" Rory waves to the pink-haired, young girl behind the counter, my bubbly social butterfly. "It's wicked."

"Auggie goes around telling everyone it was his first commissioned piece–"

"It wasn't?" Mouth gaping open, Rory's floored. "Auggie's a fuckface sometimes, but not a liar."

"He lies worse than I do," I blurt out before I can stop myself, then worry about the can of worms I've opened, since Rory is a gossip-hound. Ignoring Rory for a second, I make a beeline to the counter.

"Hello." I use my *trust me, I'm Officer Devon* voice. "I have tactile issues, object fixations, and tics, so I can't wear my wedding band. I was wondering if you do walk-ins? Nothing major, just a wedding band tattoo."

Leaning over the counter to get into my personal bubble of space, the girl shows off her many, glittery rings on her fingers. "Do you spin it a lot?" She spins her own ring around her finger, causing a visceral reaction within me.

Rory tugs me away from the counter, getting between the girl and me, then leans on his hip, all relaxed like. "Hyper-focused, Devon practically sawed off his own finger by twisting his ring and rubbing at it. His therapist gave us the go-ahead, saying Dev will view the tattoo as an extension of his own skin, not as an intrusion."

"That's hella cool." The young girl looks at me, eyes roving from my head to my toes. "My brother's like that." Only the younger generation will think me *cool*. The elderly janitor at the Batcave calls me a freak to my face on a daily basis.

"Dave!" the girl bellows toward the back, giving me a chance to look around. It's just an empty annex, not even a chair to park your ass and wait. With a front desk acting as the bouncer to the business end of things, and thousands of intricate designs papering the walls.

"Dave's my brother." The girl nods her head, like we have a network, and we'll automatically recognize one of our own kind. "We just opened up a few minutes ago. Early in the day, it's pretty dead in here. But, late at night… booked solid, all the way down the block."

"We're in luck," Rory stage-whispers, all chipper. "That means I can get my cherry popped too."

"Oh, my God!" her voice pitches higher with an upward inflection. She can't be more than fifteen at the most, reminding me more of Essie and Beth at that age, instead of my raven-haired baby sister. "You're too hot to be a virgin."

"I meant a tattoo," Rory deadpans, keeping a straight face. I physically have to turn around, and cover my face with my palms, to stop myself from barking wildly with laughter.

"That too, hun– far too hot to not be wearing ink." I swear to God, the girl swoons on top of the counter. "You're hot too, twitchy… but this man–" she fans herself.

Rory turns to me, mouthing, "*Twitchy?*" no doubt fearing I'll go postal. But I don't, because teenagers are still kids, and they're entertaining as fuck.

Leaning in, doing a little stage-whispering of my own, "I can attest to the fact that this hot man is definitely *not* a virgin." … and that's when the tattoo artist enters the front, just as his baby sister swoons off her stool.

Eyeing us, and then eyeing his sister, the tattoo artist is nothing as I expected. I was waiting to get my ass handed to me by a big, burly tattooed guy, wearing leather pants, and a biker's beard. But he's no bigger than I am, maybe thirty at most, with thick, black-rimmed glasses. No leather, no beard, but covered up to his neck in a kaleidoscope of tattoos.

"Percy," he warns in a parental tone. "What'd I tell you about being flirtatious with the customers?"

"Only if they're under eighteen." Percy pouts out her lower lip, eyes never leaving the six feet and several inches of Rory's perfect frame. "But no one under eighteen comes in here, 'cuz they can't get a tattoo yet."

The tattoo artist winks at me, managing to keep his expression stern. "Catch-22… just mind the front desk." Turning to Rory and me, "I'm assuming the big guy is over eighteen. How about you?"

"This must be what it feels like when a woman over thirty gets carded," I murmur wryly, not knowing if the guy is jerking my chain or not. "I'm twenty-one, happily married, and have a baby on the way."

"He's also a cop," Rory pitches in, not helping matters.

Head tilted in Rory's direction, I openly stare at him in confusion. Who in their right mind would drop that little ditty in a tattoo parlor, of all places. Then I notice how Dave keeps checking me out, and I realize Rory's acting jealous.

"The big guy–"

"*Who's not a virgin*," Dave flirts with me.

"Definitely not," I release on a chuckle. "Is twenty-five, also married, and manages a club."

"You two are interesting… follow me." Dave disappears behind the desk, Rory's eyes burning a hole into his back.

Hitching up my pantleg, I'm feeling pretty good about myself, with a sulking Rory following closely behind me. "Dave's flirting with you," Rory whispers into the back of my scalp, breath fluttering my hair. "I don't like him."

"He's harmless." Laughing underneath my breath, I wonder if Dave's actually doing us a solid, giving Rory a swift kick in the nuts when it comes to treating me the same way he does in private while we're out in public.

"Have a seat," flows to us as we enter Dave's domain– a rolling stool heads my way, courtesy of Dave hooking it with his ankle.

The place is nothing like I expected, same as with the artist himself. The walls are bright white, the floor is oversized black tiles you usually see in commercial buildings, and the surfaces are glistening stainless steel with black padded cushions on the table and stools. Even the cabinets are black and shiny. Sterile, but in a good way.

Dave's parked on a stool of his own, arm resting on a rolling table, pencil in hand. "Tell me what you'd like as your design. You can either do a mock-up yourself, or I can do it for ya."

Eyes flicking to Rory, this part is kind of private. "Do you trust me?"

Rory gazes at me with great concentration, like he's trying to bore inside my mind and steal the information. "Am I getting the same tattoo as you?"

"Yes," I state matter-of-factly. "With just a slight difference, but essentially the same. A ring tat, which you can cover with your wedding band."

"I trust you," Rory says unequivocally, eyes flicking to Dave, who he obviously doesn't trust. "I want another tattoo," he drops as a bombshell. "But I want to design it myself– I'm no artist, but I'm good with lettering."

"Rob or Auggie?" pops out before I can stop it.

"Auggie," Rory says with a quick nod. "Only time we weren't fighting was when he was teaching me to do different fonts." Stepping toward the front, Rory's feet hesitate, then he looks at me over his shoulder. "I'll go flirt with Percy while you get your tattoo, but you owe me that story about Auggie's back piece."

"Deal," is an easy negotiation. "My next tattoo, you can sit with me, but I want this to be a surprise."

"Same," is whispered, word loaded, then Rory disappears to the front.

"Boyfriend?" Dave guesses, looking as if he's trying to puzzle out the conversation Rory and I just had, and he's finding missing pieces.

Ass landing on the stool, I steal the pencil out of Dave's hand. "After you see my shitty mock-up, which you're going to have to redesign for me, your question will be answered."

*_*_*

Dave was impressed with how my simple tattoo told such a complex story. I'd found the grinding buzz of the tattoo gun a painful pleasure. I said this to Dave, and he told me many people get addicted to the endorphin rush, the wash of chemicals your brain produces during times of pain. We agreed I better stick to tattoos smaller than a fifty-cent piece to avoid another addiction, or else I'd end up looking like Dave, when it's against regulation in the department.

Acting all covert, Rory snuck into the backroom as I exited, giving me a quick kiss in passing, making sure Dave saw it. Dave promised to make sure Rory didn't watch as his band was tattooed, lest it ruin the surprise.

Now I'm hiding my hand behind my back, hanging out with Percy, Essie, and Beth in the main annex– both our girls having a look about them, as if they have a high of their own. My guess, it's the shopping bags scattered around their feet.

I said we were going to have to buy another piece of luggage and check the bag, but Beth suggested we FedEx it home, because it would be safer and more economical. That's why Beth and I are each other's cheapskate, responsible spirit animals.

"That is gorgeous!" Percy's outrageous theatrics are entertaining. She's made fast friends with the girls, who keep showing her their bargain purchases. "Aww… it's baby clothes. I want a baby."

"NO!" is a firm bark, then Dave's dark head of hair appears from the back. "You're fifteen– I'm already stuck raising you. No boys. No flirting. No crime. No drugs or drinking. No babies. Have at everything else."

"Ugh! You're such a buzzkill, Dave." Giggling evilly, while holding a onesie, "I'm going to call you Buzzkill Dave from now on."

"Better than twitchy," announces Rory's arrival, a ginormous, high as hell grin plastered across his face. "I'm quite partial to hottie, myself."

"Hey." I'm magnetized to Rory, tugging him away from everyone else, wanting to do our big reveals in private, not in front of our wives, and surely not with Percy watching on. Dave doesn't matter, not after he's the one who designed and inked the tats in the first place.

"The band is for all of us, but I wanted to show you in private." Realizing how that sounds, I motion for the girls to join us, leaving Percy to drool over the stack of purchases on the desk. I figure the clothing is safe, seeing as how Dave said no crime in his list of don'ts.

"I want to see yours," I beg, reaching for Rory's hand, while Beth and Essie try to get a look over my shoulders, both of them resting their hands on my hip and back. "I've looked at mine enough."

"No, you first," Rory states firmly, brooking no room for argument. Hardly ever does he display authority, so I give in this time.

"Okay," I breathe bashfully, holding my hand out like a newly engaged girl would, flashing off her big rock.

"Oh, my God!" is obviously from Beth, mingling with Essie's, "Aww... my heart is bursting with love."

Dave is a true artist, creating an actual metallic looking band, when all I designed was a simple script. Front and center, on my ring finger, **Essie**. The point-of-view shifts, from the front to the sides. Where the final E in Essie ends, **Rory** begins, curving around the side of my finger. Where the first E starts on Essie, **Beth** curves around the other side of my finger, their names connecting together in the back at the Y and H.

Without having to look at Rory's finger, I know exactly what it looks like. Rory's ring tattoo is the same as mine, except Beth's name is in the center, mine is curved on the right side of his finger, with Essie's on the left.

Silent, Rory unwinds the gauze that was keeping his tattoo a secret, revealing it to our ecstatic wives, who no doubt feared whether or not our bonds were as strong with them as they were two days ago.

I felt the ring would solidify each of our positions within our individual relationships, especially inside the larger partnership.

There's a lot of uncertainty, insecurity, and guilt when starting this type of relationship, but it's compounded when your male partner is utterly silent while staring down at the tattoo you designed, and he allowed it to be inked onto his hand on mere faith alone.

"We're so getting ones just like that after you pop that friggin' kid out," Beth warns, tugging Essie to her side, arms wrapped around each other like they did a lot when we were kids. "Absolutely stunning."

Sniffling, and trying to hide it, Rory looks at me with watery eyes, leaving me on the verge of losing my shit. "I got two more tattoos," he whispers softly, like it's hard for him to speak.

With all the commotion and haywire emotions, I hadn't noticed the gauze taped across the inside of his wrists. Rory pulls the bandage off his left wrist first, revealing a date from a few months ago– a date we all know well.

"Remind me to thank Auggie for teaching you how to letter– it's beyond comprehension how it looks like it's jumping right off your skin in a 3D rendering." I mutter in awe, part of me elated, and another deflating.

Our rings symbolize our connection to one another, whereas Rory's tattoo is connected to only one of us.

"Oh, babe!" Beth shouts, face glowing with happiness. Hands lifting, she cups Rory's face and pulls him down for a smoldering kiss. "You got our wedding date on your wrist. I love you so fucking much!"

Still unable to talk, emotions getting the best of him, Rory pulls away, looking terrified for some bizarre reason. Fingers shaking violently, he repeats the procedure he did with his right wrist, as he did with his left.

Today's date.

Not yesterday's date, when all four of us came together. Not the day before yesterday's date, when Rory and Beth had their reception.

Today's date.

Gasping for breath, I have to turn around and face the wall, fearing the expression on my face. Tears sting my eyes, my lungs seize, and my ability to talk is hijacked by my emotions.

"Hey." Rory steps between me and the wall. I can feel the girls touching me, talking to me, but it just melds into the rushing sound of my heartbeat filling my ears. "Did I do wrong?"

"I love you too," I blurt out, words refusing to stay inside my mouth. "I'm in love with you– I love you too." Because today's date belongs to Rory and me, and no one else.

Today's date is ours.

"Thank fuck," Rory chokes out on a relieved laugh. All we do is stare at one another, silently communicating. No big, dramatic kissing like Beth did with Rory. No clasping hugs.

Just the intimacy of looking into one another's eyes, and knowing, without a shadow of a doubt, you're on the same goddamn page– someone gets you inside and out, and loves you anyway.

The next few minutes go by in a blur, as we pay for our tattoos. We each take a card from Dave, promising to stop in the next time we revisit Sin City for our anniversaries. As Rory and I talk with Dave, the girls are wielding their phones, friending young Percy on Facebook, bonding over contouring and hairstyle videos.

Walking down the wide sidewalk, not bothering to part for whomever is headed our way, Rory and I are flanked by our wives, who are happily swinging their shopping bags in their outside-facing hands, their other hands snuggly fitted into ours.

"Auggie?" Rory uses as a reminder, and I pretend I don't know what he's talking about.

"We're not supposed to be focusing on Auggie right now," Beth warns from her side of Rory, not being privy to our earlier agreement. "But, if it helps, I called to see if he was doing okay."

"Who here hasn't called?" Essie demands from my side, releasing an ironic chuckle underneath her breath. "I called Willow."

"I called Dad," I admit without hesitation, anything to keep Rory from interrogating me.

"I called Rob," Beth mutters like it's no big deal we all broke our promise.

"I called Auggie," Rory whispers for only me to hear. "Now tell me about his goddamn back piece, before I get frustrated."

"Uh-oh," Beth sings, laughter filling her voice. "Rory's gonna Hulk out on us. Better spill the deets."

"Back piece?" Essie tugs on my hand, gaining my undivided attention, and I know there's no escaping this now.

"Okay," I grumble, rolling my eyes. "Auggie loves to go around saying that wicked tattoo on his back was his first commissioned illustration."

"It's not?" Even Beth is shocked. "Holy shit."

"Yes, it was his first piece sold... to his *dad*," I stress, hiding my laughter.

Never piss off your little sister, especially when she's a drug addict. Because Tina spilled every sordid secret the Kline family had in their closets, while we were high out of our gourds, inside the drug den across from Rush.

"But the funniest part of it– well, not funny, it's actually kinda gross –it was *Lisa's* design."

"Lisa?" Essie and Beth say in unison, heads hitching to look right at me.

"Auggie did it to hurt his parents, because he's a fuckface," I snarl, getting angry, hearing Tina's voice in my head. "He revised it, made it his own, and did it out of revenge. Patrick bought it for a lot of money, because it was something private between him and Lisa."

"What an ass," Essie growls. "I always knew Auggie was a rotten bastard."

Eyes flashing to connect to one another, Rory and I share a quick look, then the most ironic of ironic laughs is filling the air, Beth's joining us because she's also in the know.

"Auggie bought Rush with the proceeds." A few days nonstop around these guys, and I'm turning into a gossip whore too.

"Can you please get Tina to tell you it's okay to spill all their secrets," Rory begs. No doubt Essie's ears are perking up next to me.

This time it's Beth who gazes around Rory, eyes locking with mine. She knows the Klines' dark and dirty pasts too, but not from Auggie.

"How about we make our own secrets," I say loud enough for all to hear. We're hand-in-hand with our wives, walking back to our hotel, with all the sights and sounds Las Vegas has to offer around us. "Think of the possibilities."

"I did promise to make life interesting." Rory's hand slips into mine, holding my hand in public for the very first time, completing the chain between all four of us. "For at least the next seventy years."

• EPILOGUE • SPOILER-WARNING •

Due to an intersecting storyline, Wager (Blended #7) & Polished (Rusty Knob #4) share the same Happily Ever After epilogue. If you read both series, or plan to read both series, I'd suggest not reading farther unless/until you read both books first.

If you don't read both series, continue onward, knowing there may be slight confusion as four characters are shown (characters briefly mentioned in the later chapters of Polished, but not in Wager due to the timeline). Their story has no direct impact on this journey, just characters from another series lending an ear while discussing the pitfalls of living in a polyamorous relationship.

If you read both series, never fear– this message, and the following epilogue, will be word-for-word in both books. Whichever book you read first, you don't have to go back to it to read the epilogue, just continue forth to read the Happily Ever After for both sets of characters.

Thank you for being patient and understanding… with the flip of the page, enjoy the epilogue.

· THE FUTURE · FAIRPORT, MASSACHUSETTS ·

After a Double-Wedding

EPILOGUE- A REAL ONE, NOT JUST THE LAST CHAPTER

3rd Person Narrative
(Yeah, Erica Chilson's going there for once)

Rusty Knob meets Blended in the final of finales. **In the distant future**, the Blended series has just met its end, with readers wondering if Ms. Chilson will ever revisit for the next generation, and the Rusty Knob series has probably been concluded many books ago. M&M of Restraint is probably still kicking, with the 100+ characters the author accidentally created.

Readers will never know, because this is Erica Chilson, and she does what she wants, when she wants, but this is the outcome she has envisioned since the beginning… Will it change? Doubtful. Maybe. Quite possibly… you'll have to wait and see.

Some of Rusty Knob's cast came out in support of Francis Parker, forgoing quick flights for a road trip. Bren and Jack, with Jesse and Libby, loaded the kids into a minivan, and wanted to murder each other somewhere in the middle of Pennsylvania. Honor pulled the van over, told everyone to get out, and forced them to have a time-out on the side of the road. When the adults were behaving– no longer baiting each other –the kids let them back in the van.

A first honeymoon of their own, Penny and Warren will regret leaving their teen children alone for a week, learning Copper is just as conniving and intelligent as Grandpa Corbin, and Ginger is just like her parents when it comes to keeping her panties on. Never fear, Aunt Willa is scary when the neighbors seek her out in hopes of shaming her for letting her kin run wild.

The grooms from the double-wedding are flying high in the sky toward destinations Erica has yet to decide on. Francis Parker and Sage Fischer, best friends forever, but they surely aren't marrying each other– their grooms are also best friends forever, popular even outside of Fairport's circles, but you'll have to wait until the final book in the Blended series to find out… oh, and in case you fear Ms. Chilson is creating a trend– never fear, they don't share.

Dan and Uriah were hanging out in their larger apartment, right in the heart of Pittsburgh, exhausted after Ransom and his husband thankfully gathered their children after their special day with the uncles. Neither man has ever wanted to procreate, not with Ainsley and Ransom filling the world with more Bishops, and Uriah's siblings via his godmother are quite randy. Their rest was short-lived, because Wynn and Kade showed up to stuff them into a very large, and equally expensive, SUV, maxed out with the latest tech and all the creature comforts of home.

Their road trip was amazing, filled with many touristy stops along the way. Wynn was waylaid in Amish Country by woodcraft. But once they hit New England, every stop promising *real* maple syrup had Kade, Dan, and Uriah groaning like little kids asking, *are we there yet?*

Wynn and Kade are smarter than the average bear (Warren and Penny), and had the good sense to drop their kids off with the grandparents. Royce and Willa were happy to have some snuggles, since the twins have flown the coop and Brynn is lonely without siblings to harass. No fear, a broody Copper was dragged in by his ear, complaining he's an adult by Rusty Knob standards, and Penny's locked herself in Hailey's bedroom after Willa lit into her on the virtues of being a lady.

All's good in Rusty Knob, with Willa playing sheriff and Royce as her deputy.

Here, in Fairport, agreeable kids are tucked in beds, with the older Mason, Prynne, and Kline spawn roaming the streets as a gang of artists and misfits. The adults are also tucked in bed, either fast asleep or having a second honeymoon of their own.

Bren and Jack lied to Libby– the more gullible and agreeable of the mothers –saying they were going out with the boys, sticking Jesse and Libby with the kids for the night. Hiding out in a hotel room, Bren and Jack put the **Do Not Disturb** sign on the door, and plan to not come out until late tomorrow morning.

Clustered around the living room, in a rehabbed drug den, across the street from Rush, Polyamory Not-Anonymous meets face-to-face for the first time. After years upon years of online communications, and random phone calls, they finally meet those who offered comfort and support from afar.

"I wish we had people like us when we were younger." Essie's in a plush recliner, rocking a chubby baby. "Well, we had Robin."

"Robin!" Beth and Rory huff out in a laugh on the loveseat, with Devon's, "Tweety!" echoing from near their feet.

The wine is flowing, so Devon found a place on the floor– the grown man is kneeling by the coffee table, putting together a 500-Piece puzzle Maeve wants to hang in her bedroom – confusing the four men dominating the sofa.

Kade and Dan are cuddled in the center of the sofa, with Wynn and Uriah butted up closely to their sides, holding their hands. They may be confused, but they are also amused by how this house is run.

No surprise, Devon is obsessive, to the point he bought the house that changed his, Tina, Tom, and Taryn's lives. Devon bought the house and the lot next to it, Willow's company renovated it with several additions and an at-home practice for Beth, and Essie flawlessly planned to move eight people into it. Rory was pleased with the commute, a thirty-second jog across the street to get to work at Rush.

Devon and Essie, and Rory and Beth, and their four children haven't lived here long, but it's been a struggle to adapt, especially socially.

"At some point, you just have to go with your gut and not give a shit anymore when the townsfolk try to shame you." Devon looks up from his puzzle, pinning the four guys on the sofa. "I've broken most laws I was sworn to uphold. I've repented, but our relationship is the one thing the town holds against me. Do you see how ridiculous that is?"

"Gay!" Kade, Wynn, and Uriah blurt out, raising their hands, with Uriah finishing it out. "Even in today's day and age, gay is all people see. Especially allies, believe it or not. *I'm going to support Uriah's magazine because he's gay*, not because it's a great publication spreading information on LGBTQ issues. Like I have a handicap attached because of my sexual orientation and my nonbinary gender. I want my work to stand beside all the rest and be judged on its content– sometimes they toss in my ethnicity too."

"Woman!" Beth and Essie chirp at the same time, then giggle at one another.

"I understand, Uriah– I do." Beth reaches across the coffee table to pat the man's thin thigh. "Certain men are allowed to accomplish things without a disclaimer attached, and the rest of us aren't. Female and gay Olympiads– *the wife and mother won the gold medal*," Beth twists out in a commentator's voice. "Sometimes going as far as to give the husband's name first. *The gay diver broke a world record.* When just a man wins, his name is the subject of the announcement, and his achievement is the predicate, and there is no mention of his sexual orientation, ethnicity, gender, his relationships, or his children. He owns his accomplishments, not a large grouping of people or the husband and kids in his life."

"Oh, my God." Essie leans forward, adjusting the baby in her arms. "Remember when I won an award from the Fairport County Chamber of Commerce?"

Rory leans forward to take the little fella from his mother's arms. As the youngest of the children– Essie's last baby, since she had a tubal to ward off Devon's incessant need to procreate– Devon Junior is fair of hair and eyes, the spirit and image of the man holding him.

Incidentally, there is another little boy sleeping soundly in his bed upstairs. Rory Junior. Beth's only child is dark of hair with the darkest of blue eyes, and isn't the spirit and image of his namesake or his mother's husband.

The children's origins cause much speculation and censure among the pitchfork carrying townsfolk.

"Instead of the article being about Primp and Essie, it started off with the Mason legacy of law enforcement, listing John, Malcolm, Devon, Ozzy, all the way down to Violet, and mentioned the future generations they hoped to join the force." Cradling the baby to his chest, Rory looks down at Devon for a split-second before continuing with what he was saying.

"Then Weston was brought up, listing his entire football career– but it did add he was the *gay* co-head of Fairport School

District's athletics department," Rory mutters wryly, squeezing his son to his chest.

"Oh, my God!" Essie throws her hand up in the air, causing everyone in the room to grin at her theatrics. "Then the article talked about Lucky Clover's, and all the foodservices it provides, never saying Clover's name at all. Then Ren and Wreck & Ruin–"

"My favorite was how they said your parents were wintering in Florida," Beth taunts Essie, earning a feminine growl in response. "Then they mentioned the kids, how Will is on the honor roll–"

"They never mentioned Essie until the last line of the article." Devon places a puzzle piece, focused and concentrating on the task at hand, not how there are too many people invading his personal space and the scent of alcohol riding the air. "Essie won an award for her mentoring and scholarship programs, and that was never once mentioned in the article. Essie's accomplishment was connected to everyone but her, as if she didn't do it– earn it herself."

"You're shitting me." Uriah leans forward, eyes narrowed with a glare, enraged for not only Essie, but the industry he loves so much. "Does this press have a physical location? Because this is the first time I've wanted to commit an act of vandalism."

"Cop!" Everyone but Uriah shouts, pointing at a grinning Devon.

"Don't worry about me– I'm sure my son has some spray paint somewhere." Another piece is set. "Colin caught Will, John, Opie, and Avi in the act last week. Crime spree for the untouchables. They were spray-painting a poem, of all things, on the basketball court at the little school. They were wooing Ian."

"Ah," Beth coos, an expression of pure happiness on her face. "That is so sweet, following in their parents' footsteps."

"Little too incestuous for my liking," Essie interjects, seeming terrified for her oldest child and baby brother-in-law. "Ian's a complication we don't need."

Beth's still advocating, "Ian and Opie are trying to get to know each other–"

"But wherever Penelope is, Will and John are sure to follow. I love Opie, and I want her to get to know Ian, but I don't want those boys around him."

"Lord knows what they're up to tonight," Rory mutters underneath his breath, looking proud of the mischievous new generation of Masons, Prynnes, and Klines. "Maybe they found a boombox at Revamped, and they're camped out in Ian's front lawn, reenacting a 1980s teen flick."

The newcomers on the sofa are leaning forward, soaking in every word, not knowing what any of it means, but are simultaneously relieved their lives are simpler, yet entertained by the drama playing out.

"And they say incest is a West Virginia thing," Wynn breathes into Kaden's ear, and a booming laugh filters through the living room.

"Yeah, this is deeply skirting incest, especially considering Ian's paternal line, *but the lines don't cross*," is directed at Essie in a tone that brooks no room for argument. "Our oldest son and my youngest brother, they're only a few weeks apart in age." Devon continues working his puzzle, able to be focused on one task while engaging in another, using it to keep his mind from spiraling out of control and the anxiety from rising.

"They spend every second together– it's not gross." Devon levels another look at his wife. "It's emotional, nothing sexual or romantic. After growing up around and in polyamory, they don't have the same views on relationships as everyone else. Opie and Avi's parents are in a triad. Our children in polyamory. My baby brother, John doesn't view the world like most do, even if his upbringing is traditional... so when this kid popped up on everyone's radar– I'm not going to get into the hows and whys – Will and John don't fight over him, and Ian's more confused than the rest of us."

"They're just wooing Ian into their gang– welcoming him into the fold and into the family." Rory puts his large paws over his son's ears. "They aren't trying to screw him."

"*Yet*," Essie bites out in a mother lion voice, not having it one bit.

Uriah bends forward to look across Dan and Kade at Wynn. "Remember when you laughed in our faces for saying we didn't want kids–"

"Yeah, but–"

"No, buts," Uriah stresses, gaze never disconnecting from Wynn's. "We have your kids, and our nieces and nephews– that's plenty… don't give me any more bullshit about being lonely in our old age without grandkids."

"We'll just spoil yours," Dan mutters wryly, eyes flicking to Kade. "Share in their accomplishments. Less drama, less cost, all the benefits."

"Yeah, but…" Wynn flashes Kade a pleading look. "Don't you want to see yourself in them?" Gesturing at Rory holding Devon Junior, son a miniature version of his father.

"You don't have any biological kids," Dan points out. "You only wanted Kade's, remember?"

"Well, maybe I want yours too," Wynn blurts out, and a second later he looks horrified. "Shit! I mean, look at Uriah– who wouldn't be interested in what his child would look like." Wynn backpaddles, face a wash of embarrassment. "I didn't just mean Dan's kids, by the way, even though that's how it sounded. I've been pressuring both of them. It's like I have a biological clock ticking down, but it ain't mine."

"Welcome to our world," Rory sings, voice filled with amusement. "You came to us for advice, and that's the most important we can give."

"What's your dynamic?" Beth interjects before things get dicey. "We have very clear lines in our relationship, and I'm curious about yours. No one ever wants to be honest when I ask."

"It's not something easy to talk about." Wynn's face turns to the side, refusing to meet anyone's gaze. "We're too worried about hurting anyone's feelings, or being rejected."

"I always knew I'd marry Essie someday." Devon stops sorting pieces to sit upright and stare at everyone on the sofa. "I was in the husband and wife mindset, where you've only bedded each other and no one else ever. It was society's picture of family and morality. But it didn't fit, no matter how hard we were forcing it– I don't mean our marriage. The mindset. When Rory and I first fit together, it was a struggle to come to terms with it."

"I was an insecure wreck, not gonna lie." Essie reaches for her son, needing a comfort object. "But then I realized, I had my best friends with me, and my husband was happy instead of hurting, and I let those insecurities go."

"I felt guilty," Rory pipes in, hand landing to rest on Devon's shoulder, fingers squeezing lightly. "I felt like I had to choose between my wife and my best friend, fearing it would destroy all four of us."

"It took *years*," Beth stresses. "We were living separately, struggling to find our place in the lives of the children we didn't bear, as if we weren't in one relationship. We eventually figured out we have several relationships inside a large partnership. The house, the kids, the accomplishments, the hurts and joys, they belong to *all* of us."

"About those several relationships..." Kade trails off, hand wavering to-and-fro, guilt obvious to anyone with eyes and ears. "What's yours?"

"You gonna tell us yours?" Beth volleys back, smirk flirting with her lips. "It's a romantic and sexual relationship between Rory and me, Devon and Essie, and Devon and Rory. Essie and I are best friends, and any girl out there will tell you that's a bond that no one can tear apart– it matters, and it's important."

"What about between you and Dev?" Uriah tries and fails to keep the tumultuous emotions out of his voice. "Rory and Essie?"

"Devon and I, we're best friends," Beth admits without hesitation. "Always will be– have each other's backs. But we're too much alike to forge a romantic connection. Not gonna happen."

"Do you have sex?" Dan's more than curious. "With Devon being demisexual?"

"We fuck, and it's good," Devon says outright, not caring there is a baby with impressionable ears in the room. "I love Beth, would never hurt her, and see her as my partner, but I'm never going to be in love with her, and I refuse to force it."

"Same!" Beth swats Devon upside the head, smirking down at him. "Don't force it."

Chill, Devon doesn't retaliate. "I was an atheist, but it was the kids that changed that for me. We'll get to Beth and Rory's struggles in a bit... but it was realizing God had a plan for us, that the four of us needed to come together, or my son sleeping upstairs wouldn't exist, and the baby in his mother's arms wouldn't either. Rory and Beth wouldn't be parents. No matter what society says, we were supposed to be together."

"I would like to know the struggles now, if you don't mind." Wynn is hyper-focused on children, and will do anything to avoid admitting feelings.

It's Beth's turn to be uncomfortable, face turning away, a sniffle echoing around the room. "I had a goal, and nothing would stop me. After I got my master's degree, I kept going for my PhD. I started my practice– we have a small garage in the back lot for me, but back then we didn't. I work with patients, but also with clients in our private club. I didn't realize fertility and age go hand-in-hand. I'm an educated woman, *obviously I knew*, but it didn't hit until it was too late."

"Even if we had tried when we first got married, it wouldn't have mattered, little pup." Rory pulls his wife into his arms, comforting her. While feathering kisses against her hair, he explains. "By the time Dev and Ess were pregnant with their second, we decided we wanted to try."

"Best friends, remember?" Beth's watery eyes and quivering smile has Rory holding her tighter. "I wanted to carry a baby at the same time as Essie, do all of that together, have our kids grow up together. That's a best friend thing. By the time Maeve was born, I still hadn't gotten pregnant."

"We did fertility testing, and Beth took hormones." Rory hides his face against the top of his wife's head, tears obvious in his voice. "By the time Will was eight or nine, and Maeve was four, we still couldn't get pregnant."

"It was *us*," Beth stresses. "Together. My body was attacking his sperm, no matter what meds I took to combat it. Fertilization was impossible. We tried IVF, and my body rejected the embryo."

"I always knew I'd put a kid in Beth's gut." Dev's words are harsh, almost unforgiving, but he takes over because Rory and Beth are too upset to continue. "Always knew it. Beth and I didn't have sex together for all those years they were trying– didn't want an oops. Maybe it was frustration, or anger at the world, but

Beth didn't turn me away when I came to her in bed, and it took a long time to get pregnant, especially for a Mason."

Varying reactions of amusement and irony echo throughout the living room, with Beth's snort the loudest.

"I get it, Wynn." Devon looks across the room and connects with the other man. "You want biological children with the ones you love. Rory and Beth can understand how bittersweet it is to not share that. I feel it too, wanting children with Rory, and knowing it's a biological impossibility. So I gave my son Rory's name, a son grown inside his wife, and we did the same for the baby in my wife's arms right now... I get it."

"It's romantic between Essie and me." Rory continues to massage Devon's shoulders, sensing his emotions are going off the charts. "We're just built softer, I guess. It's hard to be with someone day-in and day-out, share a bed and children, and not be in love with them."

"So it doesn't bother any of you how everyone is in love with Rory, Devon and Beth aren't in love with each other, and Beth and Essie are just platonic?" Uriah's like a dog after a bone, clearly upset about the dynamic in his own relationship.

"I think it's time you're honest with each other," Beth orders knowingly, voice slipping into the one she uses during counseling sessions. "Wynn, I think it's best to come from you, judging by Uriah's questions."

"Do you guys see other people outside of the relationship?" Wynn is refusing to go there, terrified of Uriah's reaction to how he feels.

"You will stop evading me before this night is out, Wynn." Beth is confident, knowing she is slowly chipping away at Wynn's reluctance. "I'll answer this, but you will owe me my answer. Fair?"

"I promise," Wynn whispers, voice cracking.

"I trust your word." Beth looks at Essie, then Rory, finally settling on Devon. Beth and Devon hold a silent conversation for several suspended seconds. Nodding, Beth continues. "Rory and Essie are happy within our home, with no need to look outside of it. However, my profession is a sticky situation."

"A therapist?" Kade drawls out, eyebrows hitching high. "We're committed to each other."

"To have sex outside of a relationship doesn't mean we're not committed or faithful," Beth chastises, tone calm enough to make you open your mind, not get defensive.

"My patients have firm boundaries. However, the work I do in our private club is more hands-on. I'm helping others, teaching them about sex, and it involves sexual contact on my part. It has nothing to do with my partners, or even me, and everything to do with the gift I was given to help those who need my help."

"You have sex with other people, but no one else does?" There's no judgment in Uriah's voice, only curiosity. "I get how with Devon it's about an emotional connection. Are you guys okay with it?"

"That's funny you should say that…" Devon trails off, with a chorus of laughter from Beth, Rory, and Essie. "I have a pass– I'll probably never use it, but I have it just in case."

"One of our friends," Essie sneaks in, amused. "It's a game Devon and Kurt play, and none of us will be mad if it happens. There's a history there, but it's private. With Beth and the Playroom, it's our life and it makes sense to us. Someone did that for us once, pushed Rory and Dev together, and Beth's returning the favor."

"We have boundaries, just like everyone else." Rory's still chuckling at Devon, who's blushing and trying to sink into the floor. "I have no desire to go after anyone else, when I have everything I need at home, and then some."

"I go with Beth." Essie glances at her best friend. "She's never alone. Sometimes the guys go too. There's a risk emotionally, since Beth is tapped into their emotions. Physically, sexually, that's another issue."

"Most of my Playroom clients are women," Beth picks it back up. "When men are involved, Rory or Dev comes with me, and Essie stays home. Safety first. It's also in a family member's home. It's not about me getting off with other people."

"Devon, on the other hand…" Rory drawls, looking simultaneously amused and jealous.

"If Kurt would give me two seconds, I'd let you join." Devon snickers sinisterly. "Besides, we got to watch Beth fuck him."

"Whoa…" Essie reaches down to slap a palm over Devon's mouth. "Private."

"*Client*." Beth shrugs it off, knowing Devon only said that because he's the jealous one. "We answered your questions, Wynn. You answer mine. What's the *actual* dynamic in your relationship."

"Obviously we're in love with our husbands." Sheepish for once, Wynn's having trouble pretending to be brave, fearing rejection himself. "Dan and Kade fell for each other first, starting with emails before their first day at college. I fucked up, and knew the only way this would work is if Dan wanted me, but that backfired."

"I wouldn't call that a backfire." Dan leans around Kade to cup Wynn's face. "It's mutual, you get that, right? I love you too, Wynn."

Breath hitching in his throat, it's evident Wynn didn't realize that, but it's Uriah's reaction that draws everyone's notice. A mournful sob is painful to hear, especially combined with the way Uriah slides down the sofa, away from everyone else. His partners stare at him, feeling utterly powerless and confused.

"Uriah," is a command from Beth. After years of conversations with all four of them, Beth is the only person who knows their fears and miscommunications, but is dutybound not to share their innermost truths, even if it was used as a means to heal. "Explain why that bothered you so much."

Sucking in a deep breath, Uriah is comforted by the firm hand Beth is using with him. "We're all in love with Dan, like Rory is with you guys." Sheepish, insecurities pounding him in all directions, Uriah refuses to look anyone in the eye.

"Everyone loves Dan, and Dan loves everyone." Hand lashing out, Uriah slips his fingers to lace with Dan's. "I'm happy about that, *honest*. Kade and Wynn love each other. But…" he stammers, unable to continue.

"But where does that leave you?" Beth coaxes, everyone else in the living room falling away for Uriah. "Are you on the outside looking in? Are you only included because of Dan? If you weren't around, would it matter?"

"Yes," Uriah breathes, expression so shattered, the men in the room grimace, and Essie clutches at her chest in pain. "I know how I feel about them, but Kade doesn't like me most of the time–"

"Stop!" Kade orders, voice whipping out to slap Uriah. "Our fighting all the time isn't because we don't like each other. It's because you're a brat who plays the martyr, and I'm a spoiled-rotten headcase. We butt heads, but that doesn't mean I don't love you, Ri."

"You love me?" Uriah perks up, seemingly shocked. "I love you too, and it hurts because we don't spend any time alone together, like we did when Dan was in Connecticut. I miss that– I miss us. We all find alone time with Dan, butnotwithme…" Uriah trails off quickly, words barely audible and scrunched together.

"It's hard to find any time for anything right now," Wynn growls, clearly as upset as Uriah. "Between work, our families, our kids, our friends, and the fucking drive, I spend most of my time either missing you, or on the phone with you."

"You miss me?" Uriah's voice pitches high, only to turn into a squeal of shock as a very large hand grabs him by the front of his shirt and hauls him over both Dan and Kaden. At seventy-pounds heavier and half a foot taller, Wynn easily manhandles Uriah onto his lap.

A flurry of whispered words is thrust into Uriah's ear, only loud enough for those on the sofa to hear. Wynn pours his heart out– the fear of rejection dissipating in the face of Uriah's misery. As the words slow, Uriah melts into Wynn's arms.

"I hear it," Wynn speaks to everyone in the room. "I hear the ignorant shit everyone says, and I know it's just the tip of the iceberg. We don't flaunt it, and being visible shouldn't be considered flaunting. We've had parents protest Kade and me working with kids, saying our lifestyle is morally reprehensible. They're the perverts, getting off on spreading how it's all about sex. Why are they even thinking about what we're doing in bed?"

"I'm no machine." Kaden releases a self-deprecating laugh. "Until this road trip, it had been months since we shared a bed together." Kaden reaches over to rub Uriah's back in comfort, then laces his fingers through Wynn's resting on Uriah's hip. "I hear it too, the condemnation."

"For me, it's about the intimacy and companionship." Dan's hand joins the party, trying to erase Uriah's pain through touch. "I spend the majority of my time either anticipating when I can see them again, or missing them desperately... I never feel satisfied or happy, like something is missing."

"It's a hollow ache that never goes away, even when we're together." Wynn glances across the room, comforted in the fact that understanding is reflected back at him– Devon, Essie, Beth, and Rory walked this rocky path before they did.

"When we're together, I'm praying time slows down, so I end up spending those precious hours fearing the ache when they're gone." Wynn closes his eyes, resting the side of his face against Uriah's hair. "It has nothing to do with sex. Empty, that's how I feel most of the time, but it's how gutted I feel the instant they walk out our door that plagues me the most."

"So why do they?" Devon asks from his position on the floor, head cocked with confusion.

"Why do they what?" Wynn sounds even more confused.

"So why do they leave?" Rory answers, always jacked up to what's playing out in Devon's head. "Why do you let them leave your house? Stop them. Tell them to stay."

"Rusty Knob is our home," Kade tries to get everyone to understand. "We have roots. It's different for us, and I don't mean our families, or our children growing up where we did. The land is in our blood. We grew up poor, generations struggling to survive. The land was the only thing we had of any worth, and you never sell it, because the financial profit would be an emotional loss. Those seventy acres are all I have left of my father and grandfather– at least five generations of Marx men. We built our home on the land for Darien and Lydia– our children."

"Have you asked them?" Beth looks at Dan as she speaks to Kade. "Have you asked them if their roots in Pittsburgh matter more than their connection to you? It's understandable how you feel about your inheritance– your home."

"We're not selfish enough to ask that," Wynn butts in before Kade can answer. "I don't want the responsibility of being the one to ask, the one who caused them to resent us, knowing they wouldn't say no because it's not in their nature, not because they want to join us."

Uriah shifts off Wynn's lap to sit on the sofa cushion. "If you think it feels any different to us–"

"Then you've got another think coming," Dan mutters their private joke.

"You came here for our advice." Rory sits up farther on the loveseat, clearing his throat. "We grew up in the same town, lived blocks from each other, and felt that hollow ache you're talking about. I cannot imagine being a couple hours apart, having to drive to see each other a few times a month."

"I think we're missing the bigger picture here." Beth knows everyone in this room, inside and out, their secret fears and wants, and she's not going to tiptoe around it any longer. "We moved in together, had kids together, even though we have a platonic relationship between Ess and me, and a sexual one between Dev and me."

Always slower on the uptake, "I don't understand," Kade whispers, but it's obvious his partners are clued in.

Devon puts his puzzle pieces aside, then gazes at the occupants on his sofa with compassion. "Who cares what everyone else wants you to do? You're not broke, you're all educated, so location means squat. Stop making excuses. Stop living in stasis. Stop getting off by being in pain."

"What my husband is trying to say," Essie jumps in, because Devon is being his usual harsh self. "We're not all in love with each other, but we make it work. You guys have an advantage."

Looking around for some help, "What's that?" Kade asks, still confused.

Dan relaxes in relief, as Uriah and Wynn wear a shocked expression, looking enlivened by the revelation.

It's Dan who puts Kade out of his misery. "All four of us are in love with each other."

Thank you for reading **WAGER**. Don't miss out on what's to come…

GOOD GIRL, Willow's coming-of-age tale.
WILDLY WEDDED WIFE, Rory & Bethany's novella.
WIDOW, Malcolm & Clover's journey.
WANTON, Opal & Ginny's tasty treat.
WARPED, Devon, Essie, Kieren, & Willow's angsty tale.
WOVEN, Rory Essex's new adventure.
WAGER, Devon Mason concluding the adventure.
WICKED, Lisa Kline, going back to the origin of the Blended series as a whole.
COMING SOON! **WAYWARD**, Auggie, Isis, and Robin's emotional roller coaster ride.
…and many more to come.

ACKNOWLEDGEMENTS

A lot of work goes into writing a novel, and it isn't just by the writer herself. **My parents:** for their unconditional support. **My readers**: thank you for reading my twisted words and spreading my books to the masses. For without you, no one would've ever heard of my stories. My readers are my lifeblood. A shout out to the members of the **M&M of Restraint Group on Facebook**: thanks for the endless entertainment and inspiration. **Wicked Reads**: (in all its incarnations) **Angela G.**, thank you for taking over and making Wicked Reads better than I could have done by myself. & thank you for helping promote my work and the work of other authors. Angela? Have I told you lately how much I appreciate you? A huge thank you to the **Wicked Writer's Betas** for keeping me grounded and encouraging me to keep trudging along when I get frustrated. Your thoughts and observations are invaluable. ((Hugs)) Beta readers who helped with Wager: **Kris | Angela | Judith | Suz | Diane | Alexis |** Someday I'd love to meet you all in real life– it would be the experience of a lifetime.

ABOUT THE AUTHOR

Erica Chilson does not write in the 3rd person, wanting her readers to *be* her characters. Therefore, writing a bio about herself, is uncomfortable in the extreme.

Born, raised, and here to stay, the Wicked Writer is a stump-jumper, a ridge-runner. Hailing from North Central Pennsylvania, directly on the New York State border; she loves the changes in seasons, the humid air, all the mountainous forest, and the gloomy atmosphere.

Introverted, but not socially awkward, Erica prides herself on thinking first and filtering her speech. There are days she doesn't speak at all. If it wasn't for the fact that she lives with her parents, giving her a sense of reality, she would be a hermit, where the delivery man finds her months after expiration.

Reading was an escape, a way to leave a not-so pleasant reality behind. Reading lent Erica the courage she gathered from the characters between the pages to long for a different life. Writing was an instrument of change, evolving Erica into the woman she is today– a better, more mature, more at peace thinker.

Erica has a wicked mind, one she pours out into her creations. Her filter doesn't allow all of it to erupt, much to her relief. Sarcastic, with a very dark, perverse sense of humor, Erica puts a bit of herself into every character she writes.

I love hearing from readers. If you would like more information on release dates, works in progress, teaser chapters, and random bits of madness, please visit my Facebook Fan Page: https://www.facebook.com/thewickedwriter my website: ericachilson.com or please contact me via email: wickedwriter.ericachilson@gmail.com
DEVIANTS ONLY, if you'd like to join Erica Chilson's closed Facebook group, M&M of Restraint: https://www.facebook.com/groups/MistressandMaster/

www.ingramcontent.com/pod-product-compliance
Lightning Source LLC
Chambersburg PA
CBHW071359170626
46811CB00003B/1180